"*Mr. Riley, what do you intend to do for a week?*"

He shrugged. "I suppose I'll stay here and heal up, if you'll have me."

"Of course. I wouldn't have brought you here if I didn't intend to allow you to heal. The doctor says you have a few cracked ribs, your nose is broken, and it will probably be several days before the swelling leaves your eyes."

"Great. I should be fixed right up in time to die."

"There is no reason Dobson should have to kill you when I can offer you an alternative."

"What's that? Are you going to give me the two hundred dollars?" He sent her a mocking grin.

"I confess the thought has crossed my mind."

He shifted slightly in the bed and gave a suspicious frown. "What would I have to do?"

She drew a sharp breath. "Marry me."

TRACEY V. BATEMAN lives with her husband and four children in southwest Missouri. She believes in a strong church family relationship and sings on the worship team. Serving as vice president of American Christian Romance Writers gives Tracey the opportunity to help new writers work toward their writing goals. She believes she is living proof that all things are possible for anyone who believes and she happily encourages anyone who will listen to dream big. Email Tracey at: tvbateman@aol.com and visit her website at www.traceybateman.com

Books by Tracey V. Bateman

HEARTSONG PRESENTS
HP424—Darling Cassidy
HP468—Tarah's Lessons
HP524—Laney's Kiss
HP536—Emily's Place
HP555—But for Grace
HP588—Torey's Prayer
HP601—Timing Is Everything

Don't miss out on any of our super romances. Write to us at the following address for information on our newest releases and club information.

Heartsong Presents Readers' Service
PO Box 719
Uhrichsville, OH 44683

Or visit www.heartsongpresents.com

Everlasting Hope

Tracey V. Bateman

Heartsong Presents

For my brother, Rod.
Your best days are yet to come.
Only believe. . .

A note from the Author:
I love to hear from my readers! You may correspond
with me by writing:

Tracey V. Bateman
Author Relations
PO Box 719
Uhrichsville, OH 44683

ISBN 1-59310-181-3

EVERLASTING HOPE

*Our mission is to publish and distribute inspirational products offer-
ing exceptional value and biblical encouragement to the masses.*

All Scripture quotations are taken from the King James Version of
the Bible.

All of the characters and events in this book are fictitious. Any
resemblance to actual persons, living or dead, or to actual events
is purely coincidental.

PRINTED IN THE U.S.A.

Or check out our Web site at www.heartsongpresents.com

one

The dusty ground rose up to meet Andy with alarming speed. He landed hard on his gut, the impact forcing the breath from him like steam from a train whistle. With a groan, he twisted around to face his assailant. George, the massive bartender, snarled down at him from the boardwalk. Andy winced as a stream of tobacco juice landed inches from his head. His beat-up hat followed.

George pointed a stubby finger at Andy and squinted hard. "Don't come back, if you know what's good for you."

The giant of a man didn't have to worry about that. All the cash Andy had carried in his pocket the night before—fifty dollars and a gold piece—was gone. Plus two hundred more that hadn't been his to spend. A split-second of fear clawed at him. Mr. Dobson was going to kill him. No way could he pay back the loan now. If only his luck had held. For once.

Andy heard the rattle of a wagon just in time to scramble out of the way as it swerved to miss him. The driver shouted a curse. "Get out of the road, drunk. I'll run you over next time!"

Andy used the edge of the boardwalk for support and pushed himself to his feet. He stepped onto the wooden platform as a woman and child passed. Holding her little girl close, the woman jerked her chin and sniffed in disdain.

He didn't care how many self-righteous biddies looked down their noses at him. He was past caring about status. What did bother him was that the little girl shrank back, her innocent blue eyes wide with fear.

The curly-headed cherub reminded him of his niece, Aimee. He'd taken Aimee a little Indian doll last time he'd seen her. Had it really been five years since he'd been back to Oregon? She was most likely becoming a young lady now. He had promised to bring her another doll. Pain squeezed Andy's heart. He blinked away quick tears. He'd never hold another Indian doll in his arms again. Alive or handmade.

His stomach lurched as his night of carousing caught up to him. Through a dizzy fog, he headed toward the alley, clutching his gut, fighting to keep from disgracing himself further in public. When the retching ended, he slid down the side of the building and sat in the filthy alley. He rested his elbows on his knees and buried his face in his hands.

Last night, he'd been on top of the world. Winning at poker, the liquor making him feel in control. Beautiful saloon girls clung to each arm—oohing and ahhing over his muscles and brains. He'd found a precious few hours to numb the pain of loss. Too bad the lucky streak hadn't held up. The liquor quickly overpowered his reason, and of course, as the money stack dwindled so had his manly charms, and the girls deserted him for greener pastures.

Now, with the reality of the morning sun stabbing his eyes and heightening the pain in his head, Andy regretted not stopping when he was ahead. One thousand dollars ahead. He could have paid back Mr. Dobson and had enough left over to get a nice little start somewhere.

A groan escaped from deep inside him. Life was such a disappointment. Maybe it would be better if Dobson's thugs did find him and end his misery. As quickly as the thought slammed into his mind, a precious image eclipsed it. *Ma.* True, he hadn't seen her in a while, and he had never really done right by her, but that didn't mean he loved her any less than his brothers did. It was just that, with sons like Hank, a preacher, and Michael, an upstanding, moral man who took Ma into his home, what did she need with a no-good son like Andy? She was better off without him in her life.

The whole world would probably be better off. He'd had the thought more than once. More times than he could count, as a matter of fact, but he'd never really believed it until this moment. He'd finally reached the end of his rope. His will to live fled and, in a moment of clarity, he made a decision. He nodded to himself to cinch the deal. So that was it. There'd be no hiding from Dobson. He would face his death sentence like a man, and maybe the end would come quick. A shot to the head or heart. And then peace. *Please, God, finally peace.*

&

Fit to be tied, Hope Parker stomped after the wagon master. She wasn't accustomed to taking no for an answer, and she didn't intend to start now. Especially from this uncouth tobacco-chewing stump of a man.

"I am willing to pay double the fare to secure a place on this wagon train for myself and my children. I can be in Independence in plenty of time to—"

The wagon master stopped and turned to her. He gathered a slow breath, obviously trying to control his exasperation. "Lady, I've already told you. It ain't a matter of money or your ability to get from Chicago to Independence. It's a matter of you being a woman alone."

"But I'm *not* alone, as I've already *told* you."

"A greenhorn boy and a maid ain't exactly what I had in mind."

"Need I remind you I will also be traveling with my driver?" She motioned toward her carriage. The aging gentleman waiting for her beside the carriage door nodded.

The wagon master snorted. "Sorry, lady."

Refraining from mentioning the eight-year-old twins who would be accompanying her, as well, she squared her shoulders and matched his glare. "Perhaps I'm not making myself clear. I'm rich. I will pay anything. No matter the price."

He scowled and leaned so close, Hope had to resist the urge to retreat. But she held steady. A Parker didn't back down from anyone. And Parkers always got their way. At least when it mattered most. And this mattered. Her son's future was at stake. Perhaps his life.

"I'm telling you, lady. You could be rich as Midas and I couldn't let you on this train without a man to take care of you."

"Fine. I'll hire someone—a younger someone than my driver."

He was shaking his head before she got the words out.

In frustration, Hope stomped the ground. "Why on earth not?"

"A hired man might get sick of your bossy ways and decide the money's not worth it. Company policy. No single women are allowed space." He gave a short laugh. "If it means that much to you, go buy yourself a husband."

Hope saw red at the mockery. "I may be a plain woman, sir, but I am not that desperate. Th–there are plenty of men who want to marry me." Hated tears burned her eyes and she swallowed hard. She spun around and stomped away from the despicable man before she further embarrassed herself.

The truth was that no one wanted her. Oh, they wanted her money. She could name a half-dozen men right now who would jump at the chance to marry her bank account, but she refused to give her heart to one more gold-digger. She certainly wouldn't share her bed or her life with such a man.

Francis, her driver, opened the carriage door, and she slid onto the black leather seat, hot tears of frustration making a trail down her cheeks. She stared out the window as the carriage jostled through the street. What would she do now? She simply had to get Gregory out of this city and away from his so-called friends. At only eleven years old, her son had already had several run-ins with the law. Her money would only keep him out of serious trouble for so long before the sheriff had his fill or the judge couldn't be reasoned with.

She was just about to lean her head back on the seat and close her throbbing eyes when she noticed a scuffle in the alley. A gasp escaped her throat. Three men stood over another, obviously beating him.

She knocked on the carriage roof. "Stop the carriage, Francis!" She couldn't abide bullies. Three men ganging up on one was just too much for her already agitated mind to ignore. Reaching for her reticule, she retrieved a small pistol—a gift from her deceased husband—and exited the carriage without waiting for Francis to open the door.

"You men, stop it!" She shouted a good five yards away from the alley, knowing full well that this would draw attention from passersby. Compassion was one thing, but she was not fool enough to walk alone into an alley and confront three rough-looking men.

The men turned, dismissed her with bored glances, and returned to their task—making a bloody pulp of the poor man's face. "I said stop." She fired the pistol into the air then pointed it toward the thugs. "The next round goes into one of you. I don't care which."

"Get out of here, lady," a tall, pencil-necked man shot in her direction. "We have our orders."

"I don't care about your orders. I care about that poor man. And if you don't do as I say, I'll plug you through the shoulder then I'll send for the sheriff." She nodded toward the growing crowd. "I have plenty of witnesses."

"All right." A massive bear of a man scowled past her. Hope didn't turn around, but she could hear a crowd gathering.

"You win. But when he wakes up, tell him Mr. Dobson wants his two hundred dollars by the end of the week, or next time it ain't gonna matter how many folks are watching." The three men left through the alley in the opposite direction.

"Francis?" Feeling faint with relief, Hope turned to her driver, who looked almost as ill as she felt. "Help me get him to the carriage."

"The carriage, ma'am?"

"Yes. We can't leave him to die in the alley."

Now that the show was over, the crowd had dissipated. Resentment burned in Hope at the lack of compassion. The unconscious man weighed a ton, but they managed to get him into the carriage.

Hope pulled a handkerchief from her reticule and swiped at the blood still coming from his broken nose. He reeked of sweat and vomit, and she wondered if perhaps she'd been hasty in her decision to bring him home. After all, there was a church just down the street where she was sure he'd be welcome. When a church was called The Good Samaritan, it really had no choice but be willing to take in a wounded indigent.

A moan escaped his throat, igniting her pity once more.

"Shhh," Hope soothed, gently pushing a strand of red-brown shoulder length hair from his face. She jumped as he grabbed her wrist and buried his lips in her palm.

Hope's heart leapt in her chest. She wasn't often in the presence of such masculinity and even stinking and wounded, this man exuded a power she found exhilarating. Disconcerted by her rapid pulse and the direction of her thoughts, she pulled her hand away.

"Yellow Bird?"

Yellow Bird? He thought she was a squaw?

"Are we in heaven, my love?"

Hope swallowed hard. A man in desperate love. Oh, why couldn't anyone love her that deeply?

"Shhh," she said once more. "We'll get you taken care of. You'll be all right."

"You're not Yellow Bird."

"No."

"Yellow Bird's dead. Why? Why didn't they kill me?" The cry seemed wrenched from deep within his gut. And he passed out again.

Hope's throat tightened and she swallowed hard. What caused a man to come to the end of his rope? Was the loss of love enough to make a man give up on life? Or was there more to his story? He obviously needed something to live for.

She studied him. He was big and, given his buckskin clothing—foul though it may be—he appeared to be rustic. Just the type of man a swaggering wagon master might find suitable to "take care of her" on a westward trail.

This man was desperate. He needed to pay off that Mr. Dobson character or risk death. True, he seemed to want to die, but she highly doubted he'd want to go through another such beating.

Perhaps the wagon master had been right. If she wanted a man to accompany her west, she'd have to buy one.

two

Every inch of his body screamed with pain. Andy tried to open his eyes but the light jabbed at him, forcing him to squeeze his lids shut.

He remembered standing up and walking toward the alleyway entrance, determined not to hide like a gopher in a hole from Dobson's men. They'd found him before he'd gone ten feet beyond the alley and had pulled him back into the narrow pathway. He'd been certain the putrid ground, flanked on either side by buildings, would be his tomb.

Years of base living had flashed through his mind at the last second, and he'd hoped to wake up in heaven, or at least not in the alternate place. Waking up on earth never entered the realm of possibilities. Why was he still alive?

He forced himself to open his eyes, moaning at the pain. His lids felt heavy and barely opened wide enough for him to see though tiny slits. Dobson's thugs had done a number on him. That was for sure. Touching his eyes, he winced. They were so puffy, it was a wonder he could see at all.

He shifted, trying to find a comfortable position for his aching body. Then he noticed the pillowy-soft, warm bed. Running his hands along the crisp, clean quilt, he felt his throat tighten.

When had he stopped feeling like a man and started to accept an animalistic existence? Lying in a bed felt foreign to him. For the past two years, he'd been passing out in alleyways, and when he could get by with it, an unsuspecting farmer's barn. Occasionally, when his luck held out, he spent a few hours in a room above the saloon. Why hadn't he realized how dirty he was before now? The contrast between him and this clean bed was startling, sobering.

Ma would be so ashamed.

He was ashamed.

Andy's ears, sharp from his years of scouting for wagon trains, picked up the sound of footsteps outside his door, coming close. They hesitated and, instinctively, he reached for his guns. Panic rose inside of him. His belt was gone from his waist. Where were his guns? His vision was limited by the swelling, but he made a quick sweep of the room. The weapons were nowhere to be seen. Unaccustomed to feeling this vulnerable, Andy sat up, poised to defend himself with his bare hands, if necessary.

The door opened, revealing the intruders. He relaxed and released a pent-up breath. Two children, a boy and a girl, stood in the doorway. They couldn't be more than seven or eight years old. Irritation shot through him as they stared at him as though he were something from a freak show.

"Who are you?" he asked, gruffly.

Apparently taking his question as an invitation, the two bopped into the room, closing the door behind them. "I'm Betsy. This is Billy. We're twins. Can you tell?"

"No." Why didn't they just go away and leave him alone? Where were their parents? Children had no manners nowadays.

"Well, we are. Only we're not identical. Except we both have brown eyes and practically brown hair. And the same birthday. We're going to be nine."

"Well, my brothers both have reddish-brown hair like mine, but we're not twins."

"We are."

"Good for you." *Now, go away.*

"Woo-wee, someone busted you up good, didn't they, mister?" The little boy finally got a word in edgewise. But Andy wished he'd kept his trap shut. He didn't need a four-and-a-half-footer reminding him of why he felt like he'd been trampled by a bull.

The boy inched closer, examining Andy's wounds. "How come you got yourself thrashed? Did you steal a horse?"

Resentment burned his chest. "No. I didn't steal any horse. Only a lowdown varmint would steal from someone."

"You mean you're not a lowdown varmint?" The boy sounded disappointed.

"No."

Betsy stepped closer and gave him a scrutinizing once over. "You look like a lowdown varmint to me. Don't he, Billy?"

Andy released a frustrated breath. "Where's your mother?"

The little girl shrugged. "She had to go out. Said not to disturb you."

"Then maybe you'd better obey her."

"Naw, we'll be out of here before she gets back."

"What makes you think I'm not dangerous? What if I get out of bed and scalp you like a wild Indian?"

"You won't get out of bed."

"I might."

"No, you won't. Francis took off all your clothes. Loaned you a pair of his long johns. He said they were too little for you. But he got them on you anyway."

Alarm shot through Andy. He ran his hand over his chest. The tight, scratchy long handles were definitely not his. He hadn't even noticed. And the little girl had him pegged right. He wasn't going to get out of bed without proper clothes on. "Little girls shouldn't talk about a man's state of dress. It's not very polite."

Betsy shrugged. "It's the truth."

"It's still not becoming for a pretty little girl like you to speak of such things." Andy inwardly grimaced. Now why had he gone and told her she was pretty? From the grin on her round little face, he'd won her over and would probably never get rid of her.

"You think I'm pretty?"

Determined not to encourage the newfound friendship, he grunted and closed his eyes. "Go away. My head hurts."

He heard a shuffling and sighed. Maybe they were leaving.

No such luck. He continued to listen to water being poured into a basin then little bootsteps headed back to his bedside. Lying motionless, he pretended to be asleep. A cool, wet cloth was laid gently across his forehead, followed by a gentle kiss on his cheek. "We'll leave you alone, mister." Betsy's voice sounded close to his ear. "I'm glad you're not a varmint."

Feeling his throat clog, Andy scowled but didn't open his eyes. Just like a female. Tell her she's pretty and she either wants to be your mother or your sweetheart.

Andy didn't answer the child. He listened as the twins left, closing the door softly behind them. He had to admit the kindness had done something to him. They might be precocious, but at least they had hearts.

His unnamed baby girl would have been about two years old if she'd lived. He pictured a small child with coal black hair and large brown eyes. "Daddy!" A word he'd never hear. At least not directed at him.

Tears burned his eyes. Ma would have loved Yellow Bird. They had planned to visit Oregon as soon as the baby was born and able to travel. But the baby had been stillborn and, within three hours, Yellow Bird had followed their child in death. Ma would have loved her. He should have gone home, but grief had driven him to the bottle instead.

The cool cloth on his head was soothing and soon Andy

felt himself drifting to sleep, dreaming of his mother's smile and the gentle green fields of his Oregon home.

❧

Gathering a steadying breath, Hope pushed open the door to her guest's room. She stood at the threshold, debating whether or not to step inside.

His eyes were closed, perhaps swollen shut? Maybe that was for the best. If he couldn't see what she looked like, he might be more likely to agree to what she was about to propose.

"Excuse me. Are you awake?"

His eyes slowly came open. If you could call it that. She wondered how well he could see. Hope's stomach dropped.

"Yeah."

There was nothing to do but go inside or look foolish. Taking care to leave the door open just in case he tried something, she took choppy steps until she stood next to his bed, just out of reach.

"How are you feeling?"

"Like I've had the feathers knocked out of me."

"That's putting it mildly, I fear." Forgetting her anxiety, she reached toward the cloth on his head.

He grabbed her wrist. "What do you think you're doing? I don't like to be touched."

"Believe me. The last thing I want to do is touch a filthy gutter rat. Take your hands off me. I was just going to rewet the cloth for you."

She thought he might have blushed, but she wasn't sure through all the bruising. Either way, he let go.

"Sorry," he muttered. "Filthy gutter rats don't always have the best of manners."

It was Hope's turn to blush. "My tongue seems to have a mind of its own at times. Especially when I get mad or scared."

"I didn't mean to scare you."

"You didn't. You made me mad."

He chuckled. "Didn't mean to do that, either."

Hope enjoyed the rich sound rumbling from his broad chest. Her gaze traveled to his shoulders. What would it be like to rest her head there? Were his shoulders wide enough to bear her burdens?

"How did I come to be here?"

Jumping, Hope felt her cheeks flood with warmth. She fervently hoped he hadn't caught the direction of her gaze.

"We found you in the alley. Three men were about to send you to Glory."

"Will your man be stopping by? I'd like to thank him for saving my life."

"You mean Francis?"

"If that's your husband's name, then I reckon that's who I mean."

Hope couldn't stifle her giggle at the thought of being married to Francis. Her driver had to be in his sixties and was shorter than she was. And, though she wasn't a large woman, he probably weighed less, as well.

"What's so funny?"

"Francis is my driver. My husband's been dead for two years."

"I see. Then who. . . ?"

"I did. I'm capable of quite a lot, actually." She set her chin a notch higher. "I do not need a man to protect me." She cringed as soon as the words left her. Wasn't she about to ask him to accompany her west for just such a purpose?

"I didn't mean to imply you did. Just trying to say thanks to whoever saved my life. Apparently that person is you." Even with puffy lips, he was obviously smirking.

Fighting to keep her temper in check, Hope took the cloth

to the basin and rewet it. "The men who beat you up asked me to give you a message."

He let out a short laugh. "I can imagine what that was."

"Yes. I'm sure you can." She twisted the water from the rag and replaced it on his forehead.

"Thank you, ma'am."

"You're welcome." Settling into a chair beside the bed, she returned to the topic at hand. "The message was that if you don't pay a Mr. Dobson two hundred dollars by the end of the week, you won't get off with just a beating next time."

His chest rose and he leaned his head back against the headboard, his eyes closed as he expelled a breath. "What would you do if you only had one week to live?"

The question startled her. He was just giving up? Didn't the man have any gumption? Or was he only outwardly strong? "I don't know. I suppose I'd do everything in my power to ensure my children would be properly cared for."

He lifted his head and captured her gaze. "Speaking of your children. You ought to teach that little girl of yours not to go around kissing strange men."

The blood drained from Hope's face. "What do you mean?" she managed to croak.

"Those twins of yours came in here like I wanted their company. Made my head hurt worse."

"Bother your head, what a—about the kiss?"

"Oh, Betsy gave me a wet cloth and kissed me on the cheek." Then, he seemed to understand Hope's fear. He scowled. "I didn't ask for either. I'm not that low."

Offering no apology, Hope met his gaze evenly. "Well, a mother can't be too careful. Especially one who is raising her children alone."

He nodded. "Then maybe you shouldn't bring strange men into your house. You never know what sort folks are, and that little girl is too pretty and too sweet to be left at home when there are strangers in the house."

Sweet? "Are you sure we're talking about the same Betsy?" She couldn't resist a smirk. Obviously, this man was a pushover for a little girl's attention. Recognizing his concern for what it was, she dismissed her fear that he might be out to harm her child. He might be a drunk and a slacker, but he was no monster. Of that, she was sure.

Betsy had softened a place in his heart already. He couldn't be all bad. Perhaps he could be reasoned with to enter a mutually beneficial relationship with an uncomely woman.

"The men called you Andy. But I'm not comfortable addressing you as such. What is your last name?"

"Riley."

"Mr. Riley, what do you intend to do for a week?"

He shrugged. "I suppose I'll stay here and heal up, if you'll have me."

"Of course. I wouldn't have brought you here if I didn't intend to allow you to heal. The doctor says you have a few cracked ribs, your nose is broken, and it will probably be several days before the swelling leaves your eyes."

"Great. I should be fixed right up in time to die."

"There is no reason Dobson should have to kill you when I can offer you an alternative."

"What's that? Are you going to give me the two hundred dollars?" He sent her a mocking grin.

"I confess the thought has crossed my mind."

He shifted slightly in the bed and gave a suspicious frown. "What would I have to do?"

She drew a sharp breath. "Marry me."

three

Andy bolted upright, catching the soggy cloth as it slid from his forehead. The woman wanted him to. . .

"What did you just say?"

Clearing her throat, she leveled her gaze at him. "Marriage would fix both of our problems."

"How do you figure that?"

Her shoulders rose and fell as she made an obvious effort to steady herself. "I'll be honest with you Mr. Riley. I want to travel west, but the wagon master won't allow me to go unless I have a husband."

"Wagon master? Last I checked, wagon trains don't go through Chicago."

"That's true. But even mean-spirited wagon masters have families they want to see from time to time. Francis attends services with this one's sister. That's how I heard he was in town and that he's leading a train to Oregon in two months. Of course we'd have to travel by steamship to Independence."

Andy glanced around at the luxurious room, then back at her. "Why would you want to go west? Didn't your husband leave you with enough to live on?"

She gave a short, bitter laugh. "Yes, he left me plenty. My father also left me a fortune, and I have an honest family friend who looks after my affairs. But sometimes it isn't enough to be well off."

"It's a difficult journey. Perhaps a little too difficult for someone seeking adventure."

"This isn't about thrill-seeking, Mr. Riley." Tears pooled in her brown eyes. She clasped and unclasped her hands in her lap. "My son, Gregory, is falling in with the wrong crowd of boys. I'm afraid nothing I do is deterring him."

Bewilderment shot through his veins and the sentiment found its way into the tone of his voice before he could squelch it. "You want to uproot your family because of a few boyish pranks?"

Anger flushed her cheeks, adding a spark to her eyes that Andy found quite attractive. He shook away the thought, chalking it up to her proposal. A man should be attracted to a prospective wife even if he had no intention of heading to the altar. Still, the feeling must have been subconscious, because the more she spoke, the more becoming he found her.

"My son's antics are hardly simple boyish pranks, Mr. Riley. He's smoking and drinking—"

Andy grinned as wide as his fat lip would allow. "I did those things as a boy. It's natural. He'll grow out of it."

Shooting to her feet, she waved her hands in the air and brought them back to her sides with a smack. "Oh, well. If *you* did it, I'm sure he's preparing to be an upstanding member of decent society. I mean, after all, aren't you just the picture of. . ." She stopped midsentence, her eyes widening with horror. She clapped a hand to her mouth.

Humiliation burned Andy. He wanted to find the courage to tell her that he hadn't always been the man he was today. Once he'd taken pride in himself, in his accomplishments as a sought-after wagon scout. Now, he was everything he'd always despised. And he couldn't blame this woman for her assessment. Still, seeing himself through the eyes of someone like her—a woman of influence and one he admired—made him wish she'd left him in the alley.

Clearing his throat, he nodded. "I see your point. Tell me about your boy."

"Oh, Mr. Riley." She dropped back into the chair as though the strength had been stolen from her legs. "He's been in trouble so many times I've lost count. It's costing me a fortune to bribe the judge to keep the foolish boy out of jail every time he runs afoul of the law. And he's only eleven years old. What happens when he gets a little older?"

Andy's lips twitched at the thought of her stomping up to the judge's bench and slapping down a bribe.

"You think it's funny?" Her eyes sparked with anger once more, and she left the chair with a flounce. "Never mind. You're not the man I had you pegged to be."

"Simmer down. First of all, you don't know me well enough to peg me any sort of man. And if you did, I doubt you'd get it right."

She blushed, and Andy once more felt the attraction to her. Irritation bit at him, and he scowled at his foolishness.

"Well, you don't have to growl at me!" Her lip trembled.

He'd done that out loud? That beating must have rattled his brain more than he originally thought.

"I'll leave you to rest, Mr. Riley." She spun around, sniffing, apparently trying to hide her tears. "Mrs. Smythe will bring your supper in a little while."

"Now, wait just a minute."

Slowly, she turned back around, hope glimmering in her eyes.

"Marriage is serious business. Why can't we just *pretend* to be a happy couple? Then I could leave once we reach the Platte. Or sooner if you're sick of my company by then. Which you probably will be."

"I'm not a liar, Mr. Riley."

He couldn't hold back his mocking laughter. "Live by the Good Book, do you?"

"What do you mean?"

"You know, thou shalt not lie?"

"Oh, the Bible." She crossed her arms. "You're the last person I'd have thought would want to wed a churchgoing woman."

"I couldn't care less."

"Then why'd you bring it up?"

"Me? You're the one who brought it up."

"I most certainly am not!"

He released an exasperated breath. "You said you wouldn't pretend to be married because you won't lie."

"Yes. And it has nothing to do with a religious affiliation. I just don't happen to believe a liar is worth his or her salt."

"You're not a Christian woman?"

She drew herself up straight and lifted her chin. "I do not hold to any denomination. I find the whole idea to be a crutch for weak-minded individuals who refuse to take responsibility for their own actions. A person can be moral and upstanding without a book to tell her what is or isn't right."

Jaws of unease crunched at his insides. He had never had much use for religion himself, but to discount the foundation on which his ma built her life seemed wrong somehow. "My ma would disagree with you."

"And what about you? Do you also disagree?"

"I don't care if you go to church or not."

She gave a clipped nod. "Fine. Now that that's settled, would you care to hear the rest of my proposition?"

"There's more?"

"Of course. There would be terms surrounding our so-called marriage."

"So-called?"

Her look grew haughty and disdain spewed from her lips. "I have no intention of sharing my life with another man."

Andy observed her, and the more he watched her, the more

intrigued he became. She was a walking contradiction. Sniffling one moment, declaring independence the next.

"If you don't intend to share your life with a man, maybe you shouldn't go around proposing marriage."

"I don't go around proposing marriage. You're the first man I've ever... Oh, forget it. I'm not going to justify my actions to a man who had to be rescued from an alley. Here are the terms. The marriage will be legal and binding. I have already transferred enough funds to private accounts so that no one can leave me penniless—say a man given to gambling." She gave him a pointed look.

Heat moved up Andy's neck. "A wise decision, most likely," he said dryly.

She lifted her brow in obvious surprise then went on as though he hadn't spoken. "I will fund the trip west and pay you to stay on through the first harvest."

"That'll be almost a full year after you reach Oregon."

"I'm aware of that, Mr. Riley. I will need a man to help build my home and teach us how to farm." She frowned. "D—do you know how to farm?"

"Not according to my brother, Michael," he said with a self-abasing grin. "But my ma thinks I do all right."

Relief crossed her features. "That's good to know."

"So you're proposing that I essentially become a hired hand for the time it takes to get to Oregon, get settled, and bring in the first harvest?"

"Not essentially. A hired hand is exactly what you'd be. I will not share a bed with you, if that's what you're implying."

"I wasn't."

Twin spots of scarlet stained her cheeks. "Oh."

She recovered quickly and once again became all business. "I have a handbook by a Captain Randolf B. Marcy called *The Prairie Traveler*. I have studied the book in great detail and am quite familiar with the supplies we'll need to procure. Francis will accompany us west. Therefore, I will purchase three wagons. You and Gregory may share with Francis. I will share a wagon with the twins and Mrs. Smythe, though Billy may be offended at the thought of sharing with two females. No matter. He'll have to accept it. The third wagon will, of course, carry supplies."

Waiting until she stopped rambling and took a breath, Andy rushed forward with his own thoughts. "I'll sleep under the stars." What was he saying? He'd agreed to no such arrangement. Not yet, anyway.

She blew out a frustrated breath. "Mr. Riley, if you sleep under the stars, who will keep Gregory from sneaking out in the middle of the night?"

Andy's heart constricted with compassion. "If I agree to this, I give you my word your son will be by your side when you catch your first glimpse of the lush green fields of Oregon."

She regarded him for a moment then seemed satisfied. "When may I expect your answer?"

"For sure by the end of the week." He gave her a humorless grin. "Although, if Dobson can't find me, he can't kill me."

Her soft brow rose. "They followed us when we brought you here."

What little hope Andy had held on to fled with her flat statement. His head throbbed. He sank beneath the covers and closed his eyes.

"I'll let you rest. I shouldn't have stayed so long."

A thought occurred to him. "Wait."

She was already at the door when he opened his eyes.

"I don't know your name."

"Hope Parker."

"Mrs. Parker. Thank you for not leaving me to die."

Fixing him with her earnest gaze, she shrugged. "I'm not in the habit of allowing harm if I can prevent it."

She didn't wait for an answer, but stepped through the door. He heard it click shut as he closed his eyes once more.

❧

Hope closed the door behind her. All strength drained from her legs and she leaned against the wall for support. If only Mr. Riley would agree to the marriage then everything would work out.

"Ma'am?"

Francis's voice startled her, nearly sending her through the roof. She flattened her palm against her stomach. "Mercy, Francis. You scared me."

"Beg pardon. But I was here when you stepped out. If you'd turned your head you would have seen me."

Something about his grim tone raised Hope's suspicions. "How long were you standing there?"

"Long enough to hear your plans. And may I say I am disappointed in your proposition to a stranger?"

"Why, Francis!" In all of his years of service, the servant had never once hinted at insolence. Still, given his long-standing status in the house, she felt he deserved an explanation. "The wagon master will not grant us a place on the wagon train unless I'm married. Even a male servant doesn't qualify us."

He looked insulted. Hope hurried to clarify. "It isn't your age. Trust me. It's my marital status. Some hogwash about company policy not allowing single women to travel alone."

"But you'd not be alone. The children and I are accompanying you."

"Trying to reason with the wagon master was like appealing to the backside of a horse. He refused to waver."

"Then might I make an alternate suggestion?" Francis

ducked his head, but not before Hope noticed his face had suddenly gone red. He twisted his hat in his gnarled hands.

Placing her hand on his arm, she smiled fondly. "What is it, Francis?"

His faded green eyes met hers. "I know I'm not nearly good enough for a woman such as yourself, but rather than giving your hand in marriage to a stranger you found in the gutter. . ." He swallowed hard. "I'd like to offer myself to you."

A gasp escaped, despite efforts to prevent it. Hope stared in disbelief at the aging servant. "What do you mean?"

"I'm asking you to marry me. Surely you see that it would be better than joining yourself to that man." He jerked his head toward the door and the lines in his face crunched together into a scowl.

"Oh, Francis." Although she knew in her heart that any marriage, to Francis or Mr. Riley, would be a farce, she needed someone who could help her build a home and get a good start on a farm. Francis hadn't lived on a farm in forty years. He would never do. But how did she tell the dear man such a thing without destroying his pride?

She lifted her gaze to his. His eyes flickered with. . .was that *anger*? Surely, she was mistaken. In his years of service, she'd never seen Francis angry. She glanced again. The careful mask of deference had returned.

"I understand, ma'am. No need for you to say anything else. I beg your pardon for forgetting my place." Giving her no chance to respond, he inclined his head and walked away.

With some regret, Hope watched the set of his shoulders. She'd wounded his pride. Thankfully, not his heart.

Releasing a weary sigh, she pressed the back of her hand to her forehead. Now what was she going to do about those twins? They'd disobeyed by going into Mr. Riley's room while she was out attending to business. She'd gone to find Mr.

Dobson and pay the two hundred dollars. Otherwise, she feared the men might break in and slice Mr. Riley's throat while he slept. This was the only way to ensure he would be alive long enough to be of any service to her.

She'd long since given up on the notion of marrying for love. Her first marriage had been to a man twice her age. Her dying father's wish in order to secure her financial future—marry his best friend and business partner. A man she'd grown up calling "uncle" and his first wife "aunt" before her untimely death.

Silas had been a wonderful uncle but a not-so-wonderful husband. He was stingy and emotionally cold. She'd never fancied herself in love. But his stinginess had paid off handsomely. She now had her father's inheritance as well as her husband's, and she would never want for anything. Anything but the love of a strong, good man. Since her husband's death, she'd received gentlemen's attentions from time to time. But her bank account was the obvious draw.

Mr. Riley seemed riddled with emotional pain, and he was a drunken gambler to be sure. But, perhaps, the heart he'd shown beneath the shaggy beard and filth was as big as it seemed. If only he'd have pity on her plight and agree to the marriage. . . .

If she were a praying woman, now would be the time she'd beg for mercy. Instead, she left the prayer unsaid and simply put her hope in Mr. Riley's desire to live. If he indeed had that desire. For now, he didn't need to know he was safe from harm. He only had to realize they needed each other. She'd been used enough by men seeking her fortune. For once, she would use a man to give her what she wanted—a future for her children.

four

The second full day Andy lay in bed, he began to shake. By the third evening, he needed a drink so badly, he clutched his bruised side and climbed out of bed in the dead of night. He tiptoed through the house barefoot in search of something to calm his nerves.

Mrs. Parker had confessed to not being a religious woman, so where was the polite drink of society? Brandy, rum, even wine? He slid his tongue across cracked lips in anticipation.

Wrapped in a blanket to cover his long johns, he shuffled through the house from room to room. After a frustrating search, he bit back a groan. Not a drop was to be found. No decanters filled with the amber-colored liquid that would make the shaking stop, the pain lessen, and the fear of death ease.

Releasing a heavy breath, he headed back to the stairs, tears of need filling his eyes. Slowly and deliberately, he climbed the steps, each foot forward sending waves of pain through his body. If only he'd found the drink, the pain would have been worth it. As it was, Andy could only keep his attention focused on the soft bed awaiting him when he reached the top of the stairs.

"Shh. You're gonna wake everyone up."

Andy's ears perked up at the whispers coming from beyond the door at the top of the steps.

"Hurry up. We ain't got all night."

Senses alerted, Andy forgot about his need for a drink. His hands stopped shaking and all of his instincts reacted to the situation.

Though he'd yet to see Mrs. Parker's troublesome son, Gregory, it didn't take a scholar to realize what was happening. The boy was sneaking out again.

In a flash, Andy twisted the knob and flung open the door. Scrambling ensued.

"Hurry, Greg," a boy shouted and dove through the open window.

Forgetting his injuries—and his blanket, Andy hurried toward the window before Gregory could follow suit. He grabbed the boy by the collar and held him fast, despite the kicking and fighting. "Let go of me!"

"Not until you simmer down."

When Gregory landed a punch in his ribs, Andy roared in pain and dropped him to the floor. "Why you little. . ."

Light from the full moon shone into the room, illuminating Gregory's sneer. His face twisted in the kind of look Andy's ma would have taken a switch to him for. Andy almost wished for a nearby woodshed. This child needed it badly.

"You stink, Mister."

"Gregory!" Hope's horrified voice admonished from the doorway. Andy swung around, wincing, and met Hope's gaze in the dimly lit room. She stood in her robe and nightgown, a candle in her hand. Pink toes peeked from beneath her gown, and her chest rose and fell as though she'd been running.

"Oh!"

Heat crawled up Andy's neck as Hope averted her gaze and held out the blanket he'd flung off in his effort to apprehend the boy.

Taking the cover, he wrapped himself up. The pain around his middle nearly robbed him of breath and he groaned.

"Come, Mr. Riley," Hope said, her tone gentle. "Let's get you back to bed. You must be in a lot of pain." She turned to her son. "Gregory, take Mr. Riley's other side and let him lean on you if necessary."

"I ain't getting nowhere near him. He stinks like a dog." He scrunched his nose. "Worse than a dog."

Hope whipped around. "Keep your opinions to yourself and obey me immediately." Her sharp tone surprised Andy. Apparently, the terseness surprised the boy, as well, for he pulled himself off the floor and stalked to Andy's side. He glared up at him and pinched his nose.

"Don't worry, boy," Andy said wryly. "I can make it on my own."

"Good." Gregory flopped onto his bed.

Hope strode to the open window and shut it firmly. Tears glistened in her eyes.

Andy swallowed hard at the look of pain on the woman's face. The same look he'd seen on his own ma's face enough times—the look he'd caused just as Gregory was causing it now.

"You stay put," he said to Gregory. "I'm keeping an ear out for you and if I so much as hear you get up to use the privy, I'll be in here so fast it'll make your head spin."

Gregory shot from the bed. "I ain't scared of you."

Andy eyed the lad, recognizing the challenge in his stance, his tone, and the snarl marring his countenance. It wouldn't take much to put Gregory in his place. A well-aimed clap to the side of his head, a shove backward. But Andy knew humiliation would only make him more resentful.

Knowing he at least had to get his bluff in on the boy, Andy kept his tone deliberately calm and leveled a gaze at the belligerent youth glaring back at him. "I'm glad to hear that. Perhaps you'll mind your manners and obey your ma out of respect then. But just in case you're inclined to try and sneak out again, remember that just one door down is a man four times your size who will tan your hide if you try it."

"Now wait just a minute—" Hope spoke up, outrage clear in her tone.

Andy silenced her with a well-placed look and she hushed, taking a step back.

"Ma, are you going to let him—"

Holding his breath, Andy watched the conflicting emotions flash across her face. He hoped she'd trust him and back him up, because if she didn't, there was no way he could help her son.

She darted a gaze at Andy, then back to Greg. Her shoulders rose and fell with her breath, and she nodded. "Yes, I am. Now get yourself ready for bed." Her voice was stern, but Andy detected a slight tremble. "You will leave your door wide open, as will Mr. Riley. If he hears you move about, he will do as he's promised. With my blessing and thanks. Perhaps I will have one night of peaceful sleep knowing that Mr. Riley will not allow you to sneak out and roam the streets like a common hoodlum."

Gregory's jaw dropped open then he fixed a venomous gaze on Andy. "I won't try to sneak out."

"Glad to hear it. I'll say good night now." With a nod, Andy exited the room. As he shuffled down the hall, he heard Greg's voice, filled with betrayal. "Would you really let him whip me, Ma?"

"Son, I will do whatever it takes to make sure you do not ruin your life. You will be a man worthy of decent people if I have to tie you to your bed every night."

"But it ain't fair."

"Isn't fair," she gently corrected. "Fair is for children who have proven themselves trustworthy. Unfortunately, you have shown nothing but disrespect, disobedience, and you've demonstrated an utter lack of conscience in regard to the law.

I have no choice but to deal harshly with you. No matter how it pains me to do so."

Andy didn't hear the reply, but before he reached his bed, he'd finally made a decision. Hope Parker was a fine woman. He had nothing to lose by agreeing to the arrangement. And, for once, maybe he could do something good for someone.

Truth be told, he missed his family in Oregon, and after witnessing Gregory's bad behavior, he felt the need to try to make it up to his ma for all the pain he'd caused her in his thirty-five years on earth. Perhaps the year spent teaching Hope and her children to farm would give him that chance. He'd marry Hope, work to make a real man of her son, and try to find a reason to live again.

❧

Hold them steady, Greg. Those horses are going to run away with you otherwise."

"*You* hold them steady." Greg shoved the reins into Andy's hands. "Why do I have to learn to drive the wagon when I have a driver to do it?"

Andy gathered a slow breath and gave the leather straps back to Gregory. "Because, on the trail everyone has to do their share. Francis'll be driving the supply wagon, I'll be riding horseback most of the time, and your ma will be driving the other wagon. Like it or not, you're going to have to drive the third wagon. Now lace those reins between your fingers like this."

Hope watched the exchange between Gregory and her new husband with frustration. The boy simply wouldn't cooperate. And it was obvious Andy was losing patience.

They had arrived by riverboat two days ago after six weeks of whirlwind planning and packing everything they could take with them. She had left her estate in the hands of her attorney and friend, to be sold when she was settled and positive it would all work out.

They had secured a place in the wagon train and, with Andy's expert advice, Hope purchased all the supplies they would need for the trail. Now, only four days before the train pulled out, Hope's body already ached from the days of preparation and learning to handle a team of horses.

Thankfully, she'd brought Mrs. Smythe along to do the cooking. At least Hope wouldn't have to learn to cook over an open fire.

The thought of traveling two thousand miles across Indian lands and treacherous terrain filled her with a variety of emotions. Mostly fear. But a glimmer of expectancy rose when she envisioned the end of the trail, her boy growing strong and manly in a place absent the influences he so easily succumbed to in Chicago.

With only a few more days until they pulled out, it seemed as though they'd never get everything ready in time. Hope had located four seamstresses who were willing to work their fingers to the bone in order to supply them with durable clothing that would last until they reached their destination.

Hope chewed her lip at the thought of what might happen if the clothing didn't last. She had only rudimentary skills with a needle. She could fix a hem or patch a hole, but those were the extent of her talents. After all, she'd always had her clothing made for her.

Once again, she breathed a sigh of relief that Mrs. Smythe would be accompanying her on the trail.

"My hands are starting to hurt!"

The whine from Gregory brought Hope back to the situation at hand. She sighed.

"They'll callus over." Andy's stone-like face left no question in her mind that he was fed up. She knew full well most men would have clapped the boy's ears by now, but Andy hadn't raised a hand. She admired and appreciated his restraint.

But that wasn't all she admired about this man who had stood with her before a preacher only a few short weeks ago. She knew the marriage was a sham, but that knowledge alone didn't stop her heart from skipping a beat when he stood close to her.

Now that his bruises had faded and the color had returned to his face, he was more handsome than she'd dared believe possible. If she'd known what a good-looking man he was underneath the filth and swelling, she might not have had the gumption to ask him to marry her.

Even now, with his face twisted into a scowl, he cut an amazingly attractive figure as he stomped his way toward her. She couldn't help but admire him. He stood taller than any man she'd ever known, a good six-foot-three or six-foot-four, she'd guess. Being a tall woman, she was used to staring eye to eye with most men. Standing next to Andy made her feel feminine, protected almost, and she liked that feeling.

"The boy won't cooperate," he growled. "I'm wasting my time."

"I understand, Mr. Riley." And, indeed, who could blame him?

He seemed to lose his thunder before her calm response. The angry creases on his face relaxed. He rubbed his hand over his stubbly jaw. "All right. I have one more idea, but if it doesn't work, I'm through trying."

"Thank you."

Without another glance at her, he closed the distance between himself and the retreating boy in a matter of seconds. Hope strained to hear what they were saying, but it was no use; they were too far away. Her brow lifted in surprise when she saw a slow grin spread across Gregory's face. The boy hopped effortlessly into the wagon seat and grabbed the reins.

Making a mental note to ask Andy about the sudden change, she left the men to their lessons and went to find Mrs. Smythe to see what was on tonight's menu. Maybe she'd even lie down a bit before the evening meal.

She walked along the line of wagons, and her stomach twisted in excitement. So far, she hadn't thought much about what the journey might mean for her. She'd been too concerned with removing Gregory from a bad influence. But as she envisioned the lush green fields and snow-capped mountains, her excitement grew.

Perhaps the journey would be a new start for her, as well. A chance to be more than a rich young daughter, wife, or widow. Perhaps she could find something she was good at, something worthy of admiration.

Approaching her own fire she smiled brightly at Mrs. Smythe, who unbent before the pot she'd been stirring.

"Hello, Mrs. Smythe. Supper smells delicious."

The woman met her greeting with a grim nod.

A foreboding premonition slithered through Hope, pushing her optimism into a distant memory.

"What's wrong?"

"My back's killing me, ma'am."

"Oh, Mrs. Smythe, I'm so sorry to hear that. But Mr. Riley says we'll all toughen up in a few days."

The woman shook her head. "I can't do it, Miz Parker. I hate to pull out on you like this, but I can't go to Oregon."

Swallowing hard, Hope tried to process the statement. "Wh—what do you mean? Where will I find another cook on such short notice?"

"I'm sorry, ma'am. You've been good to me over the years and I hate to let you down. But I don't want to spend my last years cutting out a new land. That's for young people, such as you and your new man. Pioneering isn't for old women like me."

"But who's going to cook for my family?" The wretched news had a stranglehold on Hope's throat and her words barely rose above a hoarse whisper.

The cook's expression softened to compassion and she patted Hope's hand.

"You're one mighty determined woman, honey. If you can pull up stakes and leave all that luxury for months on the trail when only the good Lord knows what you're going to find on the other side, you can surely learn to cook. And in the meantime, your family will just have to eat what you put in front of them until it gets better."

Tears pushed into Hope's eyes as she realized Mrs. Smythe wasn't kidding. She honestly wasn't going to travel west with her. Her gaze sought the woman, pleading for mercy.

A gentle smiled tugged at the woman's lips. "You can do it. Put your faith in God."

Hope snorted. Was God going to come down and cook her family's meals? Was He going to get blisters on His hands driving the wagon? Was He going to walk through miles and miles of harsh land? No. No more than He miraculously put a stop to her son's hooliganism.

Hope had two strong hands and a strong body to boot. She could learn to cook. She *would* learn and by the time she reached Oregon, she'd be the best cook that ever flipped flapjacks over an open fire.

Gathering her courage, she squared her shoulders and leveled her gaze at Mrs. Smythe. "Come and draw your pay. I will provide the fare for passage back to Chicago. Feel free to stay at the house until you procure other employment. I will be happy to write you a letter of recommendation, as well."

Tears glistened in the woman's eyes. Hope wrapped her arms about her.

"I feel like a traitor, leaving you like this, Miz Parker."

Hope forced a cheery tone. "Don't you think anything of it. We'll be okay."

Only a slight tremor betrayed her confidence. But Hope Parker faced what she had to face. And when things didn't work out the way she expected them to, she found another way to get what she wanted. A little snag like suddenly having to learn to cook was not going to do her in.

five

The smell of burning meat beckoned Andy from his dreams of walking through the woods hand-in-hand with his beautiful young bride. *Yellow Bird.* Her soft, bronze skin quickened his pulse, and he pulled her against him just as a loud clanging interrupted the tender moment.

"I hate this!"

The cry of distress brought him fully awake and to the remembrance that Yellow Bird was no longer his wife. Hope was. Uneasy guilt crept through him as he dragged himself from his pallet outside the wagon opening and rubbed his eyes.

He stretched, wishing he'd been granted a few more hours of sleep. Between trying to prepare for the trek west and keeping his promise to Hope that Gregory wouldn't wander away under cover of darkness, Andy had barely slept two hours a night during the past few days. The lack of sleep was beginning to take its toll on his strength.

After taking a few moments to wake up, he joined Hope at the fire.

Smoke billowed from the skillet and Hope stood over it, waving away the thick clouds with her apron. She avoided his gaze and fanned, doing little to thin out the smoke.

"Move back," Andy instructed. Grabbing the bottom of his shirt, he used it as a glove and removed the skillet from the fire, tossing it facedown into the dirt. The smoke soon dissipated.

"I'm never going to get the hang of this cooking." Hope spewed the words rather than speaking them. She paced in front of the smoldering skillet waving her arms like a crazy woman. "We're all going to starve to death if I can't find someone to come along to cook for us."

At the catch in her throat, Andy's chest swelled with tenderness. "I don't claim to be any kind of kitchen maid, but I can rustle up bacon and eggs and some hardtack biscuits."

Hope sucked her bottom lip between her teeth and her eyes clouded with indecision. "It doesn't seem fair, with all the other things you have to do, that you should have to cook, as well."

"I don't mind." Truth be told, he'd just as soon cook the food himself and have an edible meal for a change.

Tears filled Hope's eyes and spilled over onto her cheeks. "I'm sorry, Andy. I didn't realize how difficult a job cooking could be. I just never thought about it before. Mrs. Smythe made it seem so effortless. I. . .I don't think I paid the poor woman nearly enough."

Chuckling, Andy reached out and thumbed away a tear, marveling at the softness of her skin and picking up on the fact that she'd called him by his given name for the first time in their two-month acquaintance. Hope didn't often show a vulnerable side, and Andy enjoyed it more than he would have thought possible. He was drawn to her glistening eyes, which appeared green against the backdrop of trees a few yards away. They searched his face for a moment, then clouded and looked away.

He dropped his hand. "Why don't you go and wash your face? When you come back I'll show you how to fry bacon." *Again.*

Her eyes clouded with skepticism, but to her credit, she gave a curt nod. "I'll only be a minute."

Watching her walk away, Andy's heart went out to her. He had a feeling Hope Parker wasn't accustomed to failing at something she attempted. And he had no doubt that, given time, she would master cooking, as well. In the meantime, he hoped she wouldn't be too offended if he helped out. He'd cooked over an open fire on the trail more times in his adult life than he'd had a home-cooked meal.

"Oh, no. Don't tell me she burned breakfast again!"

Betsy's voice rang through the early morning air, and Andy was sure everyone in the camp heard the little girl's cry. He hurried to the second wagon and snatched her up, pulling her through the opening in the canvas before she could embarrass Hope any more.

"Hush, Bets. You want the whole camp to hear you?"

"Did she burn the bacon again?" Her tone, though decidedly softer was just as filled with disappointment and dread. "I'm sick of burned food. I hate it."

Andy brushed a finger across her perky little nose and gave her a stern frown. "Your ma's trying her best to learn how to cook, so you show her some respect."

"Yes, sir," the little girl mumbled.

"Now take that skillet and wash it out for me. Then I'll cook us up some crispy brown bacon that will melt in your mouth."

"You're going to cook?" Betsy asked, her eyes clouded in skepticism.

"Yes, little missy, I sure am."

Emitting a longsuffering sigh, she shook her head. "I'm going to starve before we get to Oregon," she muttered, picking up the skillet and heading to the bucket of water.

Watching her go, Andy grinned and grabbed a few potatoes from the bin in the first wagon. His moving around awakened Billy. The little boy sniffed the air and gave a sleepy moan. "Ma burned breakfast again. I'm not getting up."

"Yes, you are," Andy said firmly. "And don't let me hear you saying anything to make her feel bad about it, either."

The boy sat up, his brown hair sticking out from his head

like a scarecrow's arms. Andy couldn't hold back a smirk.

"What?" Billy asked, frowning.

"Make sure you take a comb to that hair before you come outside." He grinned at the boy. "Looks like you've been running in a stiff wind."

Andy walked back to the fire. Betsy had returned with the scrubbed skillet, but Hope was nowhere to be seen. Figuring she must not want much of a cooking lesson, he went ahead and started breakfast. They had a full day ahead of them—the last day before pulling out in the morning.

He sliced some bacon and, while it cooked, he peeled and cut up the potatoes. After the bacon was done, he set it on a separate dish and kept it near the fire so it wouldn't get cold. Then, he set the slices of potato into the popping bacon grease to cook. He stepped away from the fire and folded up his pallet. He set his blankets inside the wagon shared by Francis and Gregory. The old driver's bed was empty, but Gregory's snores nearly shook the wagon.

"Time to get up, son."

Receiving no response, he reached in and shook the boy. "Let's go, Greg."

The figure beneath the quilt sat up.

Andy sucked in a breath to discover Francis had been sleeping beneath Greg's covers.

"What are you doing?" he demanded of the older man.

"I would think that's painfully obvious," Francis retorted in his habitual manner of showing contempt for Andy. "I was sleeping and now I'm waking up."

Ignoring the condescending tone, Andy motioned toward the other berth. "Where's Greg?"

"How should I know where the boy is?"

"You're using his blanket."

The surprise on Francis's face couldn't have been feigned as he glanced down at his covers. "He must have laid this over me and snuck away." A chuckle rumbled the man's chest. "A bright idea."

"Yeah, the kid's a regular genius," Andy muttered, feeling like an idiot for thinking the two of them had reached a sort of understanding yesterday.

He stalked back to the fire. "Betsy, keep stirring those potatoes so they don't burn. If your mother comes back, tell her I went looking for Greg."

"That won't be necessary, Mr. Riley." Hope's accusing glare accompanied the icy tone of her voice. Greg stood beside her, disheveled and, clearly, he'd been in a scuffle. His eyes spit rebellion; his expression dared Andy to do something about it.

Snatching Greg by his collar, Andy yanked him away from his mother and walked him back to the wagon before Hope could recover and protest. He picked him up by his shirt and belt loops and tossed him inside. "Get cleaned up and be ready for breakfast in ten minutes. We have a full day's work ahead of us."

"You can't tell me what to do!"

"Yes," he said pointedly, "I can. Francis will stay here to keep an eye on you until you're dressed." Turning to Francis, he gave the servant a look that clearly warned him not to argue.

Greg glared, all the camaraderie of the day before gone from his demeanor. Andy felt like a fool. The lad had obviously been building his confidence so he could sneak off when Andy's guard was down. And it had worked. He must have slept harder than he'd realized. And the boy had taken full advantage of it.

Stinging with wounded pride, he walked back to the fire. Betsy still stirred the potatoes, which were now a ball of mush, but at least they weren't burnt and, therefore, were edible.

He took over and spooned the potato glob onto another

dish. He set Betsy and Billy to cracking the eggs into a bowl while he scraped the potato remains from the skillet. When breakfast was finally ready, the fare included cold bacon, mushy potatoes, and scrambled eggs.

Andy found himself unable to meet Hope's gaze. He knew he'd let her down, and he felt the weight of regret knot inside his gut. All she'd asked of him was that he help her get to Oregon and protect her son. He couldn't bear the thought of seeing disappointment in one more person's eyes.

Would he ever do anything right?

a.

Hope couldn't contain her tears as she scrubbed the egg-crusted skillet. Perhaps she was making a mistake after all. It wasn't too late to pull out and go home. The wagon train was due to move out first thing in the morning, but things were looking pretty bleak for Hope. Confusion twisted her stomach into knots.

The twins were beside themselves with excitement and would be crushed if she turned back. But Gregory had already found trouble. Even in a new town. Would this be his pattern forever? Did it really matter if they moved two thousand miles away from the influences of Chicago? Apparently, bad boys were drawn to each other without any rhyme or reason.

If Gregory was going to draw those sorts of influences no matter where they went, what was the point in putting herself and the twins through the hardship? This latest development with Gregory, coming on the heels of Mrs. Smythe's resignation, had crushed what little optimism Hope possessed.

The fact that she was a miserable excuse for a cook had stolen all of her confidence. Despite all evidence to substantiate the wretched truth of the matter, she had trouble wrapping her mind around the fact that her cooking was inedible. Hope Parker did *not* fail. She did whatever it took to succeed.

So this lack of culinary ability bit her to the core. No matter how hard she tried, she just couldn't seem to get the hang of it. She wiped the skillet dry and hung it on a peg on the outside of the wagon. At least she could wash a dish. That was something, anyway. Though she had to admit she didn't much care for the chore.

Wiping her palms along the sides of her skirt, she glanced about the camp. White tents sat alongside wagons and small fires smoldered as the campers prepared for their final day before they officially became emigrants. In the wagon directly next to theirs, a young bride blushed at something her gangly husband whispered in her ear from behind. She shooed him away, feigning offense. The young man grabbed her wrist and pulled her toward him. The bride gave up all pretenses and melted against him.

Hope bit back a smile and averted her gaze to give them privacy. Young love such as theirs had eluded her. And now, she was in the second loveless marriage of her own choosing. Pushing down the melancholy, she steeled her heart against an onslaught of emotions. She had entangled herself legally in a marriage of convenience for Gregory's sake. What sort of fool was she to think that the boy would make a miraculous turnabout just because she'd sacrificed?

Climbing into her wagon, she sat at the edge of her berth and looked around the cramped quarters—her home for the next five months. She buried her face in her palms and tried to focus her raging, conflicting thoughts into something concrete. A plan of action. That's what she needed. And it had to be fast.

She had two choices. Sell the wagons and supplies she'd purchased and go back to Chicago on the next steamer up the river. Or forge ahead with her plans and hope for the best where Gregory was concerned. The choices made her head spin.

She still couldn't believe the boy had slipped through Andy's fingers last night. She knew it wasn't her husband's fault. The poor man had barely slept in weeks in order to keep Greg from sneaking out and running away as he'd threatened when he discovered Hope's plans.

She had to admit, Andy had more than paid back the measly two hundred dollars she'd paid to get Mr. Dobson to call off his thugs.

With a rise and fall of her shoulders, she considered her actions over the past weeks. What sort of a fool married a stranger and paid him to stay married to her? Especially when it appeared Gregory would be no better off, despite the two thousand miles separating him and the bad influences awaiting him back in Chicago.

Perhaps she should allow Andy an annulment and take the children and head back to Chicago. Standing, she tied the makeshift cot to the wall and started to climb down. A warm hand on her back startled her, and she let out a screech.

"Take it easy," Andy's voice broke through her panic. "I was just going to help you down."

Heat suffused her cheeks. "Wh–where's Greg?"

"Working the team with Francis."

"I'm glad you came back, Mr. Riley. . ."

"Are we back to that?"

Frowning, Hope tipped her chin and met his gaze. "What do you mean?"

The soft brown eyes twinkled as they stared down at her. "You called me Andy earlier. I thought maybe we were dispensing with formalities."

"Oh. I. . .I suppose that would be all right. Except that. . ."

He cocked an eyebrow. "Except what?

"I was actually just about to come and find you."

A valley formed between his eyes as he scrutinized her.

"Come here." His hand wrapped hers easily in its warmth, and he led her to the bench he'd crafted the first day in camp. They sat. Keeping her hand firmly in his grasp, he demanded answers with his gaze.

"I think I made a mistake coming here." Unable to bear the intensity of his questioning gaze, she stared at their clasped hands and cleared her throat. "I. . .um. . .I just think that we might all be better off if I just go back home."

His eyes narrowed. "What are you getting at?"

"Just what it sounds like. I've decided to take my children home. You're welcome to the wagons and supplies. It's the least I can do after all your help."

"What about the bad influences you were so concerned about?"

Hope chilled to his mocking tone. Her defenses rose. "Apparently Greg will find trouble no matter where he goes."

"Maybe. Maybe not." He dropped her hand. "I don't guess I can blame you. I didn't keep my end of the bargain."

Self-condemnation burned in his eyes. Hope touched his arm. "I didn't mean that. You've done remarkably well these past weeks. Sometimes you just can't run away and expect things to be any different than they were in the first place."

"I didn't figure you were running away so much as breaking a path for your children to have a better life." He captured her gaze. "I admired you for it."

And now he doesn't.

"Thank you, Mr. Riley. I'm sorry to destroy your admiration, but I see no point in uprooting the twins for a child who will most likely not change despite my efforts."

He stood and nodded. "I can see your mind's made up so I won't try to hold you. But I think you're making a big mistake. A lot can happen to change a boy in five months. I think it'll do Greg a world of good. But you're his mother. I'll start packing the gear and I'll let the wagon master know we won't be traveling with the train in the morning."

Watching him stride away, Hope pushed aside a sudden rush of doubt. Depression settled over her as she began rifling through her belongings, separating the items to keep and those they would resell.

It was for the best.

six

Andy tethered his horse to a hitching post a full block from the saloon entrance. His throat thickened as he fought an inward battle. A battle he'd thought was over weeks ago. Now it raged with a ferocity that left his gut quivering, his hands trembling as he clenched and unclenched his fists.

For the past two hours, he'd wandered through streets, on horseback, trying to find a reason to turn around and ride back to the wagon train without giving in to the temptation.

He wiped his parched lips with the back of his hand, anticipating the warm feeling of liquid amnesia. He hadn't touched the stuff since Hope had pulled him out of the alley. Once the shaking stopped and the cravings dulled, he'd had the fortitude to vow never to touch another drop. But that was when he had another purpose in life. Now that Hope and the children were leaving for Chicago, what reason did he have to keep walking the straight and narrow?

Back at the campsite, he knew the pioneers were making last minute preparations. Excited children were being put to bed by equally excited parents. All but one family who, instead of preparing for tomorrow's adventure, was spending one more night in the wagon train and would board a steamer in the morning to head back up the Missouri River. The thought sent daggers of regret through him.

Disappointment propelled him, once more, toward the sound of the out-of-tune piano music accompanied by raucous laughter. The kind of laughter born, not of humor, but of the desperate need to laugh rather than cry. Because once the crying started, there was no stopping it.

He hesitated and stared again at the swinging doors. His emotions and desires played a tug-of-war with reason and good sense.

The last few weeks had changed him. He could admit that. When Yellow Bird died three years ago, life lost all meaning. Hope and her children had redefined that meaning. For a little while.

This morning, stark reality came flashing back to him. Reality that nauseated him. Made him want to slam his fist into a wall to let out some of his frustration. Failure seemed to chase him like a wolf after a rabbit.

Perhaps he could turn his luck around once he arrived in Oregon. Back home where, hopefully, his ma and brothers hadn't forgotten about him. Tomorrow he would begin the trek west.

At Hope's insistence, he'd accepted the wagons and supplies as payment for his help over the past few weeks. Payment. Andy's bitter laugh raised a curious glance from a passing cowpoke who was headed into the saloon—no doubt to spend every penny of his hard-earned salary.

Andy hadn't needed payment. Hope had saved him, married him, and for a while, had given him a glimpse of a new life. If either of them deserved some kind of payment, she did. Now, because he'd failed to keep his promise to protect her son, she was leaving him. He'd never see Billy and little Betsy again. Even Gregory, as much as he frustrated Andy, had found a spot to call his own in Andy's life.

Tentacles of pain once again clutched Andy's heart, tearing away the last of his resolve. With purpose, he stepped toward the doors.

"Pa!"

He jerked around just as someone slammed into him.

Scrawny arms gripped him around the waist and held him tightly.

"Greg?"

"Help me, Pa! Don't let them take me."

Andy glanced up to see the sheriff striding toward him, lines of anger etched in his face. Dread burned inside of him. What had the boy done now? "Why aren't you at the wagon train looking after your ma?" Carefully, he set Greg away from him.

"Why aren't you?" Greg shot back.

Heat burned Andy's neck, but he had no time to set the lad straight. "What seems to be the problem, Sheriff?"

"This your son?" The sheriff gave them both a dubious once-over. Andy could only imagine what a contrast they made in appearance. With his dark blond hair and hazel eyes, Greg didn't even come close to resembling Andy.

"By marriage," he replied truthfully.

The man nodded. "Well, I'm afraid he'll have to come with me."

"What are the charges?"

"Stealing. And I caught him red-handed so there's no point in telling me I've got the wrong boy. The other two got away, but this one was right there with them."

"Don't let him take me, Pa. It ain't true."

"Be quiet, Greg!" Thankful that he wasn't trying to think through a whiskey-induced fog, Andy searched his mind for a solution to this predicament. He grasped Greg's upper arms and forced the boy to look him in the eye. "First thing we're going to do is go with the sheriff so I can get to the bottom of this."

Fear flashed across Greg's face. "My ma ain't going to like that."

"Well, your ma ain't here," Andy retorted. "I am. And I'd

rather go to the sheriff's office than stand out here on the street and tell the whole town about your thieving. I think your ma would be a sight more ashamed of that. Lead the way, Sheriff."

Once they reached the jail, the sheriff opened the door and stepped aside so Greg and Andy could precede him into the building. "I'm going to have to lock him up." He grabbed a large metal key and Andy heard the sound of metal clanging upon metal then the barred door opened.

"No! You can't put me in jail!" Greg latched onto Andy. "Don't let him put me in there. Please. I'll do anything you say."

Andy's throat grew thick from concern and disgust. The boy was acting like a papoose. Worse than a papoose. Most Indian babies were disciplined early on. Greg desperately needed to be taught a lesson. Disentangling himself from Greg's grasp, he nodded to the sheriff.

"Let's go, boy."

Greg backed away, his eyes wild with fright. Andy's heart went out to him, but he knew there was nothing he could do. The boy had to learn about consequences. Reaching around, he gripped Greg's arm. "Take it like a man," he said quietly.

Angling his head so that he looked up into Andy's eyes, Greg fixed him with a rage-filled glare. Raw hatred that clearly blamed Andy for the mess he was in. He jerked his arm free and sauntered into the cell. "My ma'll get me out by tomorrow anyway, then we're headed back home."

"Don't count on it, son." The sheriff banged the cell shut.

"Care if I have a word with you outside, Sheriff?" Andy motioned his head toward the door.

The sheriff nodded. Once on the boardwalk, Andy studied the lawman. "What did the boy do, exactly?"

A heavy sigh passed through the sheriff's lips. "I caught

three of them sneaking out of Gray's General Store."

Relief sifted through Andy. Anything the boys had stolen from a store could be returned to the owner. "I'd be happy to see the boy returns anything he took."

"I wish it were that easy." Shaking his head, the man leaned against the building. "Somehow those boys found out that Mr. Gray keeps a locked box of cash in a secret space under the counter. Mr. Gray claims there was over a hundred dollars in the box.

"What about the other boys?"

"I didn't catch a good look at them. I got ahold of your son in there, but the others took off lickety-split. They took the box."

Andy's heart sank. "What'll happen to the boy?"

"The judge should be through in the next couple of weeks, and he'll most likely sentence him to a juvenile reformatory somewhere."

"A reformatory?" Andy had heard about boys who went to the so-called "houses of refuge." Generally, children came out worse than when they entered such a facility.

"Be glad he has that option. Otherwise he'd go to prison along with grown men."

"There's no way you can drop the charges?"

He scratched at the stubble on his chin. "Mr. Gray is madder than a wet hen. Unless he drops the charges himself, my hands are tied." He nodded across the street to the sign indicating the store. "You're free to try to reason with him, seeing as how young your boy is and all. Wouldn't hurt to give it a shot. Just knock on the front. He lives in the storeroom."

"Thanks. I believe I'll do just that." Andy shook the sheriff's hand and said good-bye. A scowl crunched his face as he walked across the street. If the boy had to rob a store, couldn't he have used good sense and picked one that wasn't across from the sheriff's office?

He knocked on the door. No one answered, so he knocked again. With more force.

"Who is it?" The gruff voice came from within, but Andy couldn't see into the darkened store.

"Name's Andy Riley."

"Store's closed. Come back in the morning."

"Actually, I came to talk to you about one of the boys who robbed you tonight."

Silence ensued until the key slid into the door, and a bell dinged as the man opened up. "Did the sheriff find my money?"

White tufts of hair stood out from the middle of the man's head where his hairline receded. The wrinkles on his face pinched together in a scowl that Andy couldn't quite begrudge him. After all, when a man had been robbed, he had a perfect right to be angry. But Andy hoped reason might prevail over anger.

"The only boy he caught didn't have it on him."

"Well, at least one of those hooligans will spend a good long time locked up for stealing in the first place. Maybe that'll be a warning to the rest of his friends." He swiped his gnarly hand over his hair. "Not that that does me much good."

"Mr. Gray." Hoping to appeal to the man's sense of reason, Andy latched on to his last statement. "That's exactly the point I'd like to make. My boy isn't the only one involved and he doesn't have any of your money. His mother is leaving for Chicago in the morning and would be heartbroken if forced to leave her boy behind."

"Just what are you getting at?" Deep creases formed between the man's eyes. "You want me to drop the charges?"

"I'd be obliged. We can assure you that Greg won't be around town to do you any more harm."

"But that still don't get me my money back." He shook his head. "No. The boy's got to learn a lesson."

"What if restitution were made?" Andy swallowed hard. How would he come up with a hundred dollars? His mind shot to the saloon. A few good hands might do the trick. But could he really risk it when he only had ten dollars to his name?

"Well, now. I might be inclined to talk to the sheriff if I had my money back in my hands by morning."

Despite the hopelessness of the situation, Andy found himself promising to repay the full amount by the time the store opened the following day. He shot a glance toward the jailhouse then headed that way, determination guiding his steps. Before he came up with a plan to get that money, he and Greg were going to come to an understanding.

ও

A gray dawn followed a sleepless night for Hope. She'd watched Andy ride away from camp at sundown, but hadn't seen him return. Her heart sank to her toes as she surmised where his destination mostly likely had been.

After seeing Gregory safely tucked into bed with Francis' promise not to let the boy out of his sight, she had retired, as well. Her mind swam with possible futures. What if she did return to Chicago and Gregory was worse than ever? What if he straightened up and decided he'd caused her enough grief? What if she went on to Oregon? Would he be a changed boy by the time they arrived? Or would he be worse than ever?

An even worse scenario presented its horrifying image sometime near dawn. What if they were attacked by Indians and the whole wagon train was murdered and scalped. What sort of mother took her children across two thousand miles of rough terrain and hostile lands? On the other hand, what sort of mother took her troublesome son back to Chicago where he most certainly would reconnect with his bad friends?

"If You could give me some sort of sign about what I should do, maybe I'd believe in You," she whispered into the darkness of her canvas home.

A knock outside the wagon startled her, and she felt like she'd been caught stealing. She shook her head at her foolishness. She'd actually said a prayer.

"Just a moment," she called, reaching for her wrapper. When she was decent, she opened the flap. Her heart reacted to Andy's presence standing tall and handsome outside of her wagon. Gregory stood next to him. "What are you two doing together?"

"The boy has something he'd like to say to you."

"What is it, Greg?"

His face reddened considerably and he swallowed hard. Andy nudged him. "Go on."

"I. . .I just wanted to say I'm sorry for all the. . ." He paused and leaned toward Andy. Andy turned his head away and whispered. Greg nodded. ". . .grief I've caused you in my young, miserable life."

He paused again. Andy whispered again. Hope felt a giggle coming on and fought hard to suppress it.

Greg cleared his throat. "I appreciate the sacrifices you've made to make me straighten up." Pause. Whisper. Nudge. "And I think I would become a much better citizen if we go to Oregon like we planned."

Fighting hard to keep her laughter at bay, Hope regarded her son evenly. "Are you sure this is what you want, Greg?"

The boy scowled. Andy cleared his throat. Loudly. "Yes, Ma."

"It's not too late?" She turned the question to Andy.

"All the supplies are still here. The only thing is that I'm going to help drive the wagons instead of riding horseback."

"What will you do with your mount?"

Greg and Andy both stared at the ground. Now it was Andy's turn to pause. He scrubbed at the perpetual stubble along his jaw. "I. . .uh. . ."

"He sold it, Ma."

A gasp escaped Hope's throat and she looked from Greg to Andy. "But why?"

"I can't share my reason, Hope. You'll just have to trust me that I didn't get into trouble. I didn't lose it in a game or sell it for the same purpose."

He gazed at her with such earnestness that Hope couldn't question him. She decided to trust her husband. Whatever he'd done to convince Greg to straighten up had been brilliant. The boy looked more subdued than she could remember in a very long time.

She smiled at her son, and then Andy. "Well, I'd better get dressed. We have a long day ahead of us. I suppose you'd better give me that cooking lesson after all."

"My pleasure." His smile reached his eyes, making Hope's pulse race.

Flustered, she averted her gaze. "F—fine. I'll be out in a few minutes."

Without waiting for a response, she dropped the flap. A smile curved her lips as she hurriedly donned one of her new, serviceable gowns. "Wake up, sleepyheads," she called to the twins. "We're going to Oregon today!"

Billy raised his head and gave her a sleepy look. "Did you forget? We're going back to Chicago."

Ruffling his head, Hope laughed out loud. "No, I didn't forget. Our plans have changed back. We're going west. So get up so we can start the day."

Billy whooped and jumped up. "Betsy! It worked! We're

going to Oregon. It really worked!" His exuberance over-whelmed him and he flung himself into Hope's arms. She laughed.

"What worked?" she asked.

"The reverend said if we prayed and it was God's will for us to go to Oregon that God would talk to your heart and make you think it was your own idea."

"Oh, the reverend did, eh?" Indignation rolled over Hope, smothering her sudden joy. "Well, just remember it's okay for people to have their own beliefs."

"Yes, ma'am. And I believe God is sending us to Oregon just like we prayed!"

"And Ma thinks it's all her idea, just like the reverend said she would." Betsy hopped up and joined her brother's antics, jumping around the tiny space. "It's a sign!"

A sign? Hope suddenly felt cold and hot all at the same time. What had she prayed only a few minutes earlier? *If You could give me some sort of sign about what I should do, maybe I'd believe in You.*

Jerking her chin, she pulled at her hair, setting it into a firm knot at the top of her head. "And maybe I will."

"What?"

She glanced at her bewildered twins. "Never mind. Get dressed and meet me outside." She crawled toward the flap then turned back and grinned. "Today we go to Oregon!"

seven

The excitement of pioneering wore off before the first exhausting week on the trail came to an end. Now, several weeks later, the thought of spending every day for the next four months staring at the backside of a horse seemed intolerable. Cruel, in fact.

Furthermore, despite Andy's assurance that she would grow accustomed to the rigors of the trail, her screaming muscles contradicted the promise with every movement. She woke each morning with knots of pain in her legs and arms.

But she would have gladly endured whatever hardships were demanded of her if only she didn't have to cook. Not only was she a complete failure at the task, she hated every second of it. There wasn't one thing she could fix that her family deemed tasty. Indeed, her efforts were met with dread and disgust. But who could blame them?

More often than not, it was Andy who—under the guise of giving a cooking lesson—prepared the meals. This was the bane of her existence. As if the layers of dust weren't bad enough. At the end of the day, she had the humiliating experience of the entire camp witnessing her failure.

But today, she was determined not to focus on the negative issues like trail grime and bad cooking. The wagon master had presented the pioneers with an unaccustomed reprieve from the monotony of life on the trail, and she had every intention of enjoying a few hours of relaxation.

Last evening, the wagon train veered off the beaten path, camping only two miles from a small town. Though the wagon master usually stayed clear of settlements, he announced his opinion that the little band of emigrants needed a change of pace. The travelers heartily agreed and began preparing for a day to explore the countryside or roam the town.

To Hope, neither roaming nor exploring held any appeal. She'd decided to spend the day resting. She allowed Andy and the children to gallivant while she stretched out on her berth and rewarded her aching muscles with some much-needed relaxation.

The stillness of the camp was broken only by the occasional lowing of cattle or the sound of industrious men making repairs to their wagons or reinforcing axles. In the distance, she heard the strumming of a guitar accompanied by soft singing. The gentle strains lulled her to a semi-conscious state. And soon she submerged under a veil of dreamy darkness.

Tap tap tap.

Hope woke with a start and sat up quickly. Sleep-induced confusion caused her to blink and glance around the wagon, wondering why on earth she was sleeping in the heat of the day.

Then it came back to her. She stretched and smiled in guilty pleasure. The last time she'd slept in the middle of the day, she'd been ill with a raging fever.

Tap, tap, tap.

Now fully awake, Hope glanced toward the flap. "Yes?"

A woman's voice penetrated the veil between them. "Mrs. Riley?"

The name never failed to give her pause. Could she really claim the title of Mrs. *anyone* when the marriage was a sham?

"Just a moment," she called. She pulled on her boots and smoothed her hair then tied up her berth and opened the flap.

"Oh." The sight of a much-too-thin, middle-aged woman with haunting blue eyes met hers. "Can I help you?"

"Are you Mrs. Riley?"

"Yes, but I'd prefer to be called Hope."

The woman smiled, revealing the absence of several teeth. "Hope's a nice name. I'm Lucille."

Hope took the woman's proffered hand, finding herself relaxing and returning the woman's smile. "I've never seen you around before. Are you traveling with the wagon train?"

"No, ma'am." She ducked her head. "But I'd like to. That's what I've come to see you about."

"Let me climb down from here and maybe you'd best start from the beginning."

Lucille moved aside while Hope exited the wagon. Hope smoothed her skirt and smiled at the woman. She motioned toward the bench next to the wagon. Once they were settled, she turned to Lucille. "Now, what makes you think I can help you?"

Twisting her hands together, Lucille took a few deep gulps of air. Finally, it appeared she had gathered enough courage, for she met Hope's gaze, entreaty clear in her eyes. "My husband has been gone now for about three months, may he find peace for his wretched soul. I'm having a terrible time making ends meet in that one-horse town."

"I'm so sorry for your loss," Hope said, covering Lucille's hands with her own.

"Don't be sorry. I knew it was only a matter of time before he cheated the wrong man. If you want to know the truth, I'm surprised he lasted this long."

Taken aback by the woman's icy stare and equally cold tone, Hope raised her eyebrows and stared back. "What is it you think I can help you with, Lucille?"

The question seemed to bring the woman back to the present. Her words burst from her, and she squeezed Hope's hand so tightly, Hope was afraid a couple of fingers might pop right off.

A sob escaped Lucille's throat and tears glistened in her eyes. "Oh. I have to get out of this town. Start a new life somewhere. When the wagon train stopped only a couple of miles from town, I thought perhaps the good Lord had finally heard my prayer. But the wagon master won't let me come along. I have plenty of cash for supplies."

Hope nodded. "Let me guess, he told you no women are allowed to join the wagon train unless they're married."

"Yes. And marriage is obviously out of the question."

"I understand exactly how you feel, Lucille. But I still don't see what I can do."

Lucille gathered a slow breath and fixed Hope with a frank stare. "The wagon master said I might ask you for employment in exchange for a place to sleep in your supply wagon. I can provide my own supplies, but not a wagon."

"What sort of employment are you seeking?" Humiliation began deep inside Hope and released in the tone of her voice. She knew exactly what sort of employment the wagon master was referring to.

The woman's scarlet face attested to the fact. "I'm handy in a kitchen." She smiled. "Or over an open fire."

Fighting between two emotions—indignation that the wagon master had dared bring attention to it and relief that help might have arrived—Hope scrutinized Lucille momentarily, then nodded. "Tell me about yourself."

ও

Andy frowned as he stood a little ways off from the creek and watched the children squealing and splashing about the water—all the children except the Parker children, that is. Gregory had no interest in cooling off in the creek with the rest of the children, so he'd left the boy repacking the supply wagon, putting new supplies in the back, and bringing the older goods forward.

The twins sat glumly on the bank, legs crossed, chins resting on fists as they observed the merriment. Finally, unable to endure the curiosity a moment longer, he slipped from his clandestine position and strode to the bank.

"Why aren't you two swimming with the others?"

Billy angled his head and looked upward at Andy, his eyes squinting in the brightness of the late afternoon sun. "We can't."

"What do you mean? Did your ma tell you to stay out of the water?" If so, Andy would go and have a talk with her. One thing he admired about Hope was her ability to be reasonable.

"That's not it." Betsy scowled up at him, as though he were a dolt for not knowing exactly what Billy meant.

"What then?" Squatting down next to them so that they didn't have to crane their necks to see him, he tugged one of her braids.

"We can't swim."

"What do you mean you can't swim?" He and his brothers had learned to swim about as early as they learned to walk. He couldn't fathom a circumstance whereby a child wouldn't know such a basic skill.

"We never went swimming."

"Well, it's time you learned, then." Andy hopped to his feet. "Let's go."

Unabashed joy shone in both sets of eyes. "You mean it?" Betsy squealed jumping from the ground.

"I sure do."

Billy's eyes clouded. "Ah, we can't let you teach us to swim in front of all the other children. They'll laugh at us."

Andy saw their dilemma. "It's all right. We'll go down from camp a ways."

Betsy gasped. "Captain Jack said we're not to walk away from camp because of redskins."

A grin threatened Andy's lips. "Tell you what. I'll protect you if we see any Indians, okay?"

Truth be told, he had seen signs they were being followed for the past week, but felt certain it was more out of curiosity than a threat. If they'd wanted to harm the wagon train, the Indians would have more than likely attacked days ago.

But doubt persisted in Betsy's eyes.

"We won't go far," he promised. "We'll stay where we can see the others, but far enough away where they won't know I'm teaching you to swim. How's that sound?"

A slow grin split her face. "Okay."

Both children were quick studies and before long had the basics down enough for Andy to retire to the bank to dry off while he kept an eye on them. Affection stirred inside his chest as he watched them splashing and listened to their giggles.

"There you are."

Andy turned at the sound of Hope's breathless voice. The circles that had darkened the skin beneath her eyes had faded a great deal, and he returned her relaxed smile.

"You seem to be feeling better."

"I took a long nap, I'm ashamed to say."

"Nonsense. Today was for doing whatever you wanted to do. I'd venture to say the sleep did you a world of good."

She nodded. "I think so."

"Hi, Ma!" Billy called from the water. "Watch me swim!"

A gasp escaped Hope's throat. "They're swimming?"

Andy's lips twitched. "What did you suppose they were doing out there?"

"Wading." She tossed the one-word answer without taking her gaze from the children in the water. "Bravo, Billy. That's wonderful."

"Watch me!" Betsy piped in, never one to be outdone.

"My, you both are quite the wonders, aren't you?" She

clutched the neck of her dress and lowered her voice. "Are you sure they know how to swim well enough to be out that deep?"

Hearing the nervous tremor while she tried so hard to be brave for the children, Andy placed his hand on her shoulder. "Do you think I'd endanger their lives?"

She turned to him. "No. I suppose not."

"I'm fond of those youngsters of yours. You can trust me to do my level best to see nothing bad happens to them."

Almost as though she did it without thought, Hope reached up and covered his hand with hers. "Thank you, Andy. I do trust you with them. Greg's been doing so well and the twins love you as though you were their real. . ." Her words faltered and she snatched her hand away. "I'm sorry."

"For what?"

"Forgetting the true nature of our marriage for a moment. It's better if the children don't love you, isn't it? Considering the circumstances."

For an instant, Andy wasn't so sure. Family life was beginning to grow on him, but he wasn't sure if the settled-down sort of existence his brother, Michael, lived was something he could take day in and day out. He glanced at his bride. As much as he admired her spirit, he knew that was as far as it went. Every time he thought of her in terms of a wife, he remembered his beautiful Indian bride, and Hope paled in comparison. As unfair as it was to compare one woman's appearance with another's, he couldn't help himself.

She met his gaze and her cheeks flushed. Andy's stomach dropped as he realized from the flash of hurt in her eyes that she had a pretty good idea where his thoughts had been. She cleared her throat and abruptly focused her attention upon the children in the water.

"Billy. Betsy. Come on out of the water now and get dried off. Supper's about ready."

"Supper?" Andy couldn't help the surprise in his tone. "You didn't need my help tonight?"

She looked stung as she turned back to him. "No. I've hired a cook. A widow from town. She's all alone and needed a means to join the wagon train. I felt it a good solution. And I know the rest of you will agree. Apparently, my plain looks aren't the only thing that make me undesirable as a wife. But at least you and the children won't have to endure my ineptness any longer."

"Hope, I'm sorry I hurt your feelings."

Turning her full body to face him, she met his gaze, her face expressionless except for her eyes. After years of associating with thugs, gamblers, drunkards, and thieves, Andy wasn't accustomed to such unabashed honesty, and her frank stares never failed to unnerve him.

"I am well aware of my shortcomings, Andy. I know that I am not beautiful, or even pleasant to look at. I know that I am a failure at learning to produce an edible meal. But I am not a fool nor am I a silly schoolgirl, so you needn't worry about hurting my feelings. I'm not in love with you, and I'm perfectly content with our arrangement."

At a loss for words, Andy watched her whip around and stomp back toward the campsite. He grinned in spite of himself. He surely had that tongue-lashing coming.

But she was wrong about one thing. . .he found her pleasant to look at. She wasn't beautiful in the obvious sense, but she was attractive in her own right. Especially when her eyes flashed in anger such as they had a moment ago, or in merriment, which was more common. Her figure wasn't bad to watch, soft looking in all the right places. She could stir a man's blood. As he followed her with his eyes, he suddenly wondered why she didn't know that.

What sort of man had married her and led her to believe she wasn't desirable? He knew he had no right to wonder such a thing. But the thought stayed with him through the children's lively chatter as they walked back to the campsite.

The sound of her laughter reached him before he saw her, and he inwardly mocked himself for worrying about her. Apparently, she wasn't wasting time pining away over whether or not he thought her desirable.

"Who's that?" Betsy asked. Andy's gaze followed hers to a woman standing over their fire.

"Your ma hired her to do the cooking." Feeling disloyal to Hope, he clarified. "She needed a place to stay on the wagon train, so your ma decided to offer her a position in exchange for a place to sleep in the supply wagon."

Betsy and Billy exchanged looks of wonder.

"What?" Andy asked, curiosity aroused by their uncommonly subdued attitude.

"It's another miracle," Betsy breathed out in a barely audible tone.

"Yeah," Billy replied, his tone echoing his sister's.

"What sort of miracle?" Andy couldn't resist a chuckle. The twins had made no pretense of their desire for more palatable meals.

"We prayed for someone to do the cooking."

Gooseflesh rose on Andy's arms and the hair on the back of his neck lifted. A chill crept up his spine and he shivered. "You mean you prayed your ma would learn to cook?"

Billy shook his head. "No, sir. We figured it'd be easier on God if He just sent a whole different person to cook like Mrs. Smythe used to do."

"What made you think to pray about something like this?"

Betsy grinned, her eyes bright with infectious excitement. "We figured God worked it out fine for us to come west. So we hoped maybe it was His will for someone to come and cook for us."

"So you prayed for God to let us come west, then you prayed He would send a cook?"

"Yep," Betsy said, her braids bouncing around her shoulders as she gave a vigorous nod. "And would you just smell that? What is it, Billy?"

"I can't tell. But it sure smells like something good."

"Let's go find out how long before we eat."

Without so much as a good-bye, the twins ran off, leaving Andy to ponder whether the newest member of their company was a pleasant coincidence or the result of children's faith.

eight

Hope stood in the creek ankle deep, scooped up water, and rubbed it over her face and neck, enjoying the coolness after an unseasonably warm day for May.

What a relief it had been not to have to bear the indignity of her disastrous attempts to produce something edible. The children were certainly grateful. Betsy had even insisted upon saying grace. Apparently, the twins had decided that this would be a new occurrence at mealtimes.

Hope grinned into the night. She could indulge them that much. Whether Lucille's presence was a result of Divine intervention or merely a welcome coincidence, Hope couldn't have been happier to have the burden lifted from her shoulders.

Lifting her skirt to her knees, she waded another step into the water.

"You scared me to death, woman!"

Hope screeched as Andy's angry voice and the sound of boots splashing into the water broke her solitude. He grabbed hold of her arm and walked her from the water, none too gently.

"Let me go! How dare you?" She jerked away, scowling at him in the pale moonlight.

He matched her, glare for angry glare. "Didn't you hear the captain's orders not to leave the campsite?"

"If I'm not mistaken," she pointed out, "I am precisely at the location where you brought my children today for a swimming lesson."

"That was different."

Jerking her chin, Hope dropped to the ground and grabbed her stockings, her anger outweighing modesty at the moment. "I fail to see how."

Andy sat next to her, drawing a heavy breath. "For one thing, it was daytime and we were within sight of the camp. For another, I was with the children to protect them in case Indians showed up."

She pulled her boot on and reached for her other stocking. "Well, you needn't be concerned about me. I can protect myself."

"Oh, really?" He leaned in dangerously close. "And how would you do that? I don't see a gun."

Hope's heart picked up at his uncomfortable nearness. Her hands shook as she slipped on her second boot. Suddenly conscious of her hiked up skirt, she stood, letting it drop to the tips of her boots. She cleared her throat, aware that he was still waiting for an answer.

"Well, I don't know exactly what I'd do until I'm faced with the situation. But don't worry, I think quick on my feet."

Andy stared up at her from his spot on the ground. "Do you?" In one swift movement, he reached and snagged her behind the knees. Hope's arms flailed wildly as her legs shot out from beneath her. She gasped, landing hard on his lap. Strong arms encircled her.

Andy's warm breath tickled her face. She gulped, unable to move. Not sure she even wanted to.

"How would you protect yourself in this situation?" he asked, his voice husky, sending tingles down her spine.

"I. . .I don't know. I have to be on my feet t–to think quick." The absurdity of her own statement combined with the nerve-wracking closeness pulled a giggle from her throat.

He chuckled then grew serious as his gaze swept her face, resting on her lips. And almost before she knew what was happening, his head swooped downward. Warmth flooded her as his mouth took hers, all at once gentle and demanding.

New sensations coursed through Hope. She'd been kissed before, of course. But never like this. Conflicting emotions warred within her until finally she melted against him, matching him kiss for kiss. When his hands moved up her back, she suddenly came to her senses and dragged her mouth from his.

"Stop," she whispered.

"We're married, remember?" His impassioned tone was nearly her undoing. "We've both been married before." He moved forward to reclaim her lips.

Hope flattened her palms against his chest. "I said stop."

To her relief, he didn't try to hold her. She stood quickly. Turning toward the water, she drew in deep gulps of air in an effort to compose herself. Her lips still tingled, and she swiped at them with the back of her hand.

Andy gave a short laugh. "That bad, huh?"

She turned back to him. "I don't know what you mean."

"Wiping away my kiss?"

More likely wiping away the unsettling effects of his kiss.

He climbed to his feet and stood close. Her insides quivered with his nearness.

His warm hand covered her shoulder and she closed her eyes, pushing back the impulse to lean her cheek against it. "I'm sorry I forgot myself for a few minutes. I guess I just wanted you to know that I find you to be a desirable woman."

"Oh, I see. So you only kissed me to make me feel better?"

He narrowed his gaze. "First you get upset with me for kissing you, and now you're upset because I apologized? Make up your mind, do you want my kisses or not?"

"I don't need a man to kiss me because he feels sorry for me."

"That's not why—"

Giving him no chance to finish, Hope went on as though

he hadn't spoken. "Our marriage is one of convenience only. I paid your debtor and you made it possible for me to go west and make a new life for Gregory and the twins. There is nothing more to it than that."

Indeed, she couldn't allow her heart to become anymore invested than it already was.

A sardonic grin twisted his lips, and he made a lazy sweep of her figure with his eyes. "It seems to me that you're getting a lot more out of this bargain than I am. A marriage, a man's help on the trail, and a full year's worth of work once we get to Oregon. That's an awful lot for two hundred dollars."

Her face flamed and she was glad for the cover of darkness. "The deal seemed fair enough when your neck was on the line. Now you want to go back on your word?"

His lips twitched. He reached forward and stroked her jaw line with his index finger. "Not go back on, maybe just renegotiate our terms a bit."

Realizing he was teasing her, Hope jerked her chin, temper flaring. "Fine. When we get to Oregon, I'll give you an increase in salary."

He chuckled and dropped his hand. "Not exactly the kind of reward I was hoping for."

"Too bad. That's the only kind you're getting."

A twig snapped close by and Hope froze. Andy put his finger to his lips, his other hand going to his holster.

Her mind spun with the fearsome images of marauding Indians. Though the Indians were peaceful for the most part, it didn't take much to set them off. A misunderstanding. An unintentional insult.

The biggest threat seemed to be in the manner of petty inconveniences. Running the horses off during the night, stealing livestock, begging for food. These things could be easily dealt with. But who knew what a group of warlike Indians might do to a couple of pioneers caught alone in the night?

Another twig snapped and Hope's mouth went dry. Andy slipped his gun from the belt. Hope heard it cock.

"Don't shoot," a nearly panicked voice called from the bushes.

Relief washed over Hope. "Gregory, what are you doing?"

He stepped out from behind the bush. "Is it true?" By his accusing tone, Hope realized he had heard the entire conversation.

"Did you only marry her for money?" He spat the words at Andy.

"I guess you heard something you shouldn't have heard, son." Andy's tone remained calm as he studied Greg, obviously expecting the worst.

His expectations were justified as Greg sneered, leaning toward Andy, challenging him. "I'm not your son."

"Greg. Watch your tone. Whether Mr. Riley is your pa or not, he's still your elder."

He turned on her, his eyes flashing anger in the moonlit night. "You paid him to marry you?"

Standing beneath her son's disgusted gaze, Hope felt small and ashamed. And even more so when he continued his discourse. "You're no better than those women. . ."

Andy stepped forward in a flash and snatched Greg's arm. "Watch yourself, boy. I won't be held responsible for what I do to you if you finish that sentence."

Watching the exchange between the two, Hope felt like weeping. Greg and Andy had come such a long way in the past weeks. She had witnessed Greg slowly change from a bitter, rude boy to a hard-working, swarthy young man with a daily sense of purpose. Had one unguarded moment ruined all of his progress? Her heart sank to her toes at the very real possibility.

As Greg and Andy stared at each other, Hope knew that neither would back down.

"Gregory, I will not stand for you speaking to me in such a disrespectful tone. I know you're angry and shocked by what you've learned. But I want you to know, I had my reasons for doing this."

A sneer marred his face. "Because you couldn't—"

Andy stepped in once more. "Boy, you don't learn very fast, do you?"

In a nightmarish second, Greg took the initiative and stomped down hard on Andy's moccasined toe.

Andy roared in pain and grappled to regain his hold on the boy. But being adept at getting himself away from the authorities, Greg darted out of reach and ran toward the campsite.

"I'll go after him," Hope said, unable to meet his gaze.

She started to sweep past him, but he reached out and took hold of her arm. "Hope."

Suddenly weary, she released a heavy sigh. "Yes, Andy?"

"He's just a boy. He doesn't know what he's saying or understand our kind of arrangement."

"I know. Thank you for championing me. But I don't need protection from my own son. Furthermore, I am capable of meting out my own discipline."

Despite his look of astonishment, she forged ahead. "As we've reestablished this evening, our marriage isn't real. Therefore your claim to my children is not that of a father, but more like a hired hand. It isn't your place to manhandle them when they are disobedient."

His jaw tightened and he released her arm, his eyes hard as glass. "Whatever you say, boss." He tipped his hat and walked away in the opposite direction, his jerky gait evidence of his anger.

Hope straightened her shoulders. She could only go after

one of them and Greg was her boy. There was no question. A twig snapped in front of her. She smiled and turned toward the sound. "Greg, I'm so glad you came back."

But the figure that stepped from the shadows wasn't Greg. She took one look at the long black hair and high chiseled cheekbones and felt the scream at the back of her throat. His hand shot out and covered her mouth before she could make a sound.

☙

It took Andy a full hour to cool off from Hope's admonishment. He supposed it was the only logical approach to the issue of discipline, given the fact that he would be leaving after a year. It wouldn't do for the children to grow accustomed to him only to watch him leave and never return.

As much as he hated to admit it, Hope was right. He owed her an apology as much as Gregory did. He hadn't treated her with any more respect than he would have treated one of the women Greg had likened her to.

He strode back into camp long after all but the sentry fires had been doused. Making his way first to Gregory and Francis's wagon, he peeked in and nodded in satisfaction as two distinct tones of snoring were heard. At least the boy had learned enough not to run off alone on the prairie. He reached inside and grabbed his bedroll, then let the canvas lower once more.

He glanced at Hope's wagon, thought to check on her and the children, but decided against it. Let her get a good night's sleep. He'd apologize in the morning.

Memories of holding Hope in his arms assailed him as he tried to drift to sleep. Many women had come and gone for a brief hour or two above one saloon or another since Yellow Bird's death, but none had taken her from his mind. Not for one second.

His eyes popped open as he realized the woman he'd been kissing had actually been Hope. Not some figment of his tortured imagination. He wasn't sure what that meant. But there was no time for him to ponder the ramifications as Betsy's voice called to him.

He sat up and looked to the wagon she shared with her mother and Billy.

Placing his finger to his mouth, he stood and strode to the wagon. "What's wrong, sweetheart?"

"Where's Ma?"

"What do you mean? Isn't she sleeping?"

"She never came to bed."

"Are you sure? Maybe she just had to take a trip to the woods."

The little girl was shaking her head before he finished his thought.

"Her berth is still tied up. That's how I know."

Unease gnawed Andy's gut. But he patted the little girl's head, trying not to show his worry.

"Go back to sleep. I'll find her."

After Betsy was settled back into bed, Andy turned around, trying to decide his course of action. Self-condemnation screamed at him. If only he hadn't walked away from her before seeing her safely back to camp.

His mind moved toward two possible conclusions. One, she'd lost her bearings and wandered in the wrong direction. Two, the Indians he'd witnessed following the wagon train from time to time over the past days had recognized an easy target.

He'd get her back. But at what cost?

Suddenly he felt alone. Responsible. The fate of this woman—his wife—was in his hands. If he didn't bring her back, three children would be left alone in the world with a man who was to blame for their mother's fate. The weight bore down upon him, and he suddenly lifted his face skyward, remembering a long-forgotten friend.

"God in heaven," he prayed, knowing there was no time for excuses. "I don't deserve anything from You. But there are a couple of youngsters here who believe You can do miracles. If that's true, and I'm not saying whether I think it is or not, but if it is, I'm asking you to do a miracle now. Because that's the only way I'm going to be able to bring Hope back to her children."

nine

Hope's head felt like it might burst any second if she wasn't allowed to sit up soon. She'd been slung facedown across the back of a horse for what seemed like hours. Fear, combined with the trail dust, made her throat and mouth so dry, she had no saliva with which to wet her lips or tongue.

Dawn was beginning to break when they finally halted. Hope could only imagine the number of miles the group had put between themselves and the wagon train. Had they discovered she was missing yet? Would anyone come after her, or would they believe her to be dead?

Just when she thought the Indians planned to leave her on the horse while they rested, Hope felt a rough hand on her back, dragging her across the saddle. She landed hard on her feet, stumbled back, and hit the ground with her backside. The fierce looking band of warriors laughed uproariously.

Too miserable to be humiliated, Hope scowled as her gaze took in the five bronze-skinned men. "Go ahead and laugh," she barked. "If you'd been flung across a horse all night like a dead animal, you'd have a hard time standing up, too." She swallowed hard. "I need some water. Or do you plan to let me die of thirst?"

The warrior who had kidnapped her came forward and shoved an army canteen toward her. "White woman not die."

Hope accepted it gratefully and tipped it up in her hands that were still bound together at the wrist. Her throat closed up and she choked, spewing water out at her captor. He snatched the canteen from her hands. She gasped and sputtered, trying to apologize through her coughing so the Indian wouldn't take a tomahawk to her skull.

When she regained her composure, she ventured a glance at the man. He scowled and offered her the canteen once more. Deciding to leave well enough alone, Hope shook her head.

He tossed her a slice of dried meat. Her stomach lurched at the thought of eating, but she knew from the lectures the captain had given that Indians took a dim view of spurned gifts. So she nodded and yanked off a chunk with her teeth.

Emboldened by her captor's kindness thus far, Hope found her voice to ask the question screaming in her mind. "What do you intend to do with me?"

"White woman mine."

She gulped hard, swallowing the rest of the bite. "What do you mean?"

"Need squaw."

Outraged, Hope struggled until she stood. "A squaw!" Her temper flared at the man's audacity. "You intend to make me a squaw?"

The warrior thumped his chest. "My squaw."

"Never!" She stomped her foot, eliciting a round of laughter from the other braves.

He stood, barely meeting her eye to eye. For the first time ever, Hope was grateful for her uncommon height. "You my squaw!" He clapped his hand firmly on her shoulder and shoved her back to the ground.

She glared back at him, too angry to care about using good sense. "I'm no man's squaw. I am, however, another man's wife. And I have three children who need their mother."

He thumped his chest again. "Five sons. No mother. You be new mother. Have new children."

Tears pricked her eyes as she saw her new future looming before her. "Please. I already have a husband. Surely a man as—as handsome as you can find a nice Indian woman among your own people who would be pleased to marry you and be a mother to your sons."

A scowl twisted his face. "You."

"I–I will never surrender."

"Then I beat until you do."

She set her shoulders and fixed him with her gaze. "Then you will beat me every hour of every day until you succeed in beating me to death."

Fierce anger flashed in his black eyes and a vein enlarged at his temple. Just when she thought he might strike her, commotion from the other side of the camp arrested his attention. Hope followed the sound with her gaze. Her stomached flip-flopped at the sight of Andy, flanked on either side by two warriors. He stood tall and proud, and only his tight jaw betrayed his tension.

"I've come to reclaim my squaw," he announced. Hope's heart leapt. Funny how angry she'd been when the Indian had called her his squaw. But when Andy did it, she kind of liked it. And despite their precarious position, Hope felt butterflies swarm in her stomach at the thought of truly belonging to her handsome rescuer.

Her captor, the one who had claimed her, stepped close to Andy. "I take woman."

Andy sized the little man up. "And I'm taking her back."

"Your squaw?" he asked jerking his thumb toward Hope. "Yes."

"Then why you sleep on ground?"

Hope gasped. They'd been spying long enough that they knew of her sleeping arrangements?

"I like sleeping under the stars. My wife prefers a comfortable bed in the wagon."

The brave shook his head. "I think squaw too much argue.

You sleep outside so no have to listen."

A slow grin spread across Andy's mouth. "I see she's already given you the sharp edge of her tongue."

The Indian looked back at Hope, then folded his arms across a burly chest and faced Andy. "I trade her."

"I have one horse to trade. That's all."

"No, one horse not enough."

The brave reached toward one of the men holding Andy's arms. The Indian handed him a knife that Hope recognized as Andy's. Andy had been quite proud of the ivory-handled knife.

"Horse and knife for squaw."

Without hesitation, Andy nodded.

The Indian turned and stalked toward her. He jerked her to her feet and slashed the leather bindings from her wrists. He gave her a shove and she landed hard against Andy, who immediately encased her in the circle of his arm.

"Are you all right?" he whispered against her hair.

She nodded. "Are they going to kill us?"

"No. But we best get moving anyway. Indians have been known to change their minds."

While the Indians admired the knife and horse, Andy and Hope slipped quietly away on foot.

❧

Weary and dirty, Hope and Andy walked into camp by supper-time the following night. A cheer rose up from among their fellow travelers, and the three Parker children raced to their mother's side. "I knew you'd be okay, Ma!" Betsy proclaimed.

A tired smile curved Hope's lips. "You did? Let me guess. You prayed."

"That's right."

"I have to admit, I was doing a bit of that myself."

"But you don't believe in praying."

"Some events in a person's life lend themselves to hoping there is a source of power greater than oneself."

Greg jerked his head toward Andy. "He found Ma," the boy said to the twins. "Not some God."

Andy stepped forward. "I admit that I said a prayer of my own. There's not much of a chance that I could have tracked five Indians in the dead of night and found them by morning."

Andy smiled down at Betsy and Billy. "You two keep on praying for your miracles. Seems like whatever you're doing, you have the Almighty's ear."

Captain Jack came forward and stuck out his hand. "Good to have you back. I did as you asked and didn't send out a search party. But we would have by daybreak if you hadn't shown up."

"I'm obliged to you. I wasn't sure how many, if any, were watching the wagon train, just waiting for the majority of the men to ride off looking for Hope. They might have attacked and taken a lot more than just one woman."

"Well, I'm glad everything worked out the way it did." The captain looked up. "Everyone try to get plenty of rest tonight. We've lost an extra day and will push harder the rest of the week to make up the lost time."

Andy followed Hope and the three children back to their campfire.

Lucille stood beside the fire, a relieved smile widening her mouth. "I'm pleased to see you made it back with your scalp, Mrs. Riley."

"Please, Lucille," Hope said dropping wearily onto the bench. "I've asked you to call me Hope."

"Yes, ma'am. Now, you sit yourself down and relax. Supper is just finishing up and I'm going to pour you a nice hot cup of coffee."

"Thank you."

Andy watched Hope in concern. She appeared to be on the verge of tears. He debated whether to step forward and pull her into his arms, but before he could make a move, the twins sat on either side of her.

"So how'd Andy get them to let you go, Ma?" Greg asked.

"Gregory," Andy admonished. Did the boy have any sensitivity at all? "I don't think your ma really wants to talk about it."

"It's all right. Andy traded me for a horse and a knife." Her flat statement narrowed Andy's gaze.

"You mean the ivory-handled knife?" Greg asked, turning accusing eyes on Andy.

"Yes, that's the one. And considering that it was your fault your ma got captured in the first place, I figured you'd be more than happy for me to trade it."

"Sure," Gregory muttered. "I guess this means the deal is off."

Hope glanced from one to the other, her brow furrowed. "What do you mean? What deal?"

"Andy was supposed to give me that knife if I behave myself on the trail and do my chores and don't try to run away."

"I see." Hope's cold gaze studied her son. "I'm sorry to disappoint you."

Gregory's face grew red. "I didn't mean—"

Her expression softened and she reached up and took his hand. "I know you didn't. But just the same, when we arrive in Oregon, I'll order you a knife as close to that one as we can get."

Gregory shook his head. "It's okay, Ma. I don't need one." He slid his hand from hers and backed away. "I got chores to do."

Andy watched the exchange and his optimism grew concerning Gregory. Perhaps the boy had the makings of a man after all. And he liked to think he might have had something to do with that change over the past weeks.

He sought Hope's gaze to see if she recognized the boy's step forward in maturity. The eyes that looked back at him were far from warm. They were downright frosty, in fact.

Taken aback by her hostile attitude, Andy excused himself and headed for the creek to clean up before supper. Who knew the mind of a woman? Save her from a band of Indians, lose your best knife and one of Captain Jack's horses doing so, and she gave you the kind of look that clearly said you did something wrong.

❧

Hope waited until later, when she was safely tucked away inside the wagon, before she allowed the tears to fall. Andy had flat out told Captain Jack not to form a search party for her? That she wasn't important enough to risk the wagon train for?

Her heart had nearly broken at his words and even now, the memory squeezed her heart.

They might have attacked and taken a lot more than just one woman. Just one woman.

Is that all I am to you, Andy Riley? Just one woman?

From the moment he'd so bravely strode into camp and demanded her release, Hope had known she was hopelessly in love. All day, she'd wanted to tell him so, to ask him if he might consider making their arrangement permanent. After all, even if he wasn't in love with her, his kisses the night before had proven that he did care for her—at least that's what she'd thought.

Oh, how glad she was that she hadn't made the offer. . . hadn't begged him to be her real husband. What a fool she'd been to think that just because a man held her close and kissed her like he meant it, that he wanted more than a simple night in her bed.

Hope swiped at the tears flowing down her cheeks and made

a firm decision. Never again would she forget the arrangement. She alone was to blame for the kisses the night before.

Andy must have been picking up on little lovesick signals for days or even weeks. It was only natural he'd respond to them. But no more. From now on, she would treat him like Francis or Lucille. Just another hired hand.

Just one woman. She was just one woman in a crowd to him.

Swallowing another sob, she turned over and buried her face in her pillow.

She would never make a fool of herself again. When the time came for him to leave, she'd let him go. That was the bargain, and she'd never forget it again.

ten

Hope and Andy settled into a silent agreement. There were no kisses, no talk of their marriage or disciplining the children. Day after day, life became about moving forward. One step and then the next and the next, with the promise that, one day, they'd step forward and their feet would land in Oregon.

The rest of the spring passed with little incident, but by mid-July, mishaps began to befall the weary band of pioneers. Wagon wheels broke, axles wore out, and almost daily, the wagon train was forced to halt for a couple of hours while repairs were made.

Stock died from the rigors of the trail or lack of water. Some were run off by Indians. Not one family among them had been unaffected by some calamity.

Water had to be rationed, and many times, a full day would pass without a drop of water to moisten parched throats. During such times, doubts assailed Hope. Had she brought her children to the wilderness to die?

The days were endless, and Hope slept restlessly at night, always fearing lest a band of marauding Indians attack while they slept. Her clothing hung from her, until she looked like a child playing dress-up in her mother's gowns. She'd become so thin, even Andy had expressed his concern.

Toward the end of July, Captain Jack announced that they were finally past the halfway point. But before their cheers had died down, the first case of cholera broke out, bringing with it swift death and constant fear.

Quickly, the disease spread, and the wagon train was halted daily for burials. In the first week, two children, one father, and the elderly reverend and his wife succumbed. Still, the wagon train buried the dead and continued on, leaving the bereft with little time to grieve. There was no time to wait out the illness. They had to reach Oregon before winter, or they might not arrive at all.

Hope bargained with God. *Keep my children safe, and I'll believe in you.* It had worked once before. The first time, she'd asked for a sign and somehow she'd found herself on the trail. And if the truth be told, she wanted to believe. She needed something to believe in. Needed to know there was a benevolent God who loved her children more than she did. A God with the power to keep them safe. Alive.

She knew she hadn't lived a righteous life—not like most of the women in the group—so she figured she'd need to resort to negotiating. She was good at negotiating. She'd gotten her trip to Oregon by bargaining with Andy. And her bargain with God had solidified it. She hoped against hope that this one would pay off for her, as well.

But it wasn't to be. Gregory failed to show up to breakfast one morning and, with dread, Hope made her way to his wagon. She climbed inside, fearing what she might find.

He trembled beneath the quilt. "I have it, Ma." His voice was so quiet, Hope had to lean close to hear, but she knew it was no use asking him to speak up. He had no strength even to speak.

"I guess you do, Greg." She tucked his blanket closer about his shoulders. "But you'll be okay."

Shaking his head, he turned soulful eyes on her. Pleading eyes. Defeated eyes. "I'm going to die for all the bad things I done, Ma."

Tears burned Hope's eyes. She smoothed back his hair. Against convention, he'd been following Andy's example and was growing it out. His blonde tresses now fell almost to his shoulders.

"Gracious, son," she said, forcing a cheerful tone, "your hair is about as long as Andy's."

A weak smile tugged at his lips. He nodded. "I wish I'd been nice to him. Andy's a good man."

"Yes, he is."

"I'm glad you married him."

A sob caught in her throat and she forced it back. If she hadn't married Andy, Gregory wouldn't be lying here, possibly dying.

"He taught me a lot, Ma."

She wished he'd stop talking like it was over. As a matter of fact, she was going to put a stop to it this instant. She hadn't brought her son across hundreds and hundreds of miles to save him from thugs, only to see him die of cholera. She wouldn't stand for it.

"Now, listen to me, young man. You are going to fight this sickness. Any boy who can sneak out in the middle of the night, carouse all night, and run from police has the gumption to lick this disease. Do you hear me?"

His eyes were closed. He hadn't heard. Hope's stomach lurched and her heart nearly stopped at how deathly pale he looked. She placed her hand on his chest and breathed a relieved sigh when it rose and fell.

But how many times would it do that before the ragged rise and fall ceased altogether?

"Is Greg sick, Mama?"

Panic shot through Hope at the sound of Betsy's voice. She turned on the child. "Get out of here. Do you want to get sick?" Her sharp tone sent a wave of shock across Betsy's face and the little girl retreated quickly.

Hope sat back onto the wagon floor, hands in her lap, and wept. She prayed through great gulping sobs, pleading with God for her son's life.

The wagon lurched forward, and the new day began.

Resentment burned inside of Hope. How dare they move on when Greg was sick? When *her* child walked a fine line between death and life.

Greg spent the day in and out of sleep. Hope left the wagon only to empty the waste bucket along the trail. The heat inside the cramped space was stifling and by the time the wagon stopped at noon, sweat dripped from her chin and stained her armpits and chest.

She glanced up dully when the canvas flap opened.

"Hope." Andy's voice was firm, but gentle. "Come out of that sickly air. I'll sit with him for a while."

She shook her head. "He needs me."

"So do Betsy and Billy."

Fear clutched at her. "Are they sick, too?"

"No. But *you* will be if you don't take better care of yourself." He reached for her. "Come on. At least eat a bite of lunch and have a cup of coffee."

Hope nodded. "Just until we start moving again."

Andy held her hand and steadied her as she climbed from the wagon. Rather than take time for a full meal, Captain Jack had instructed the travelers to keep lunch simple and eat what didn't have to be cooked. Hope gnawed on a leftover biscuit and stared vacantly into the fire, her mind focused on her son.

"Ma?" Betsy sat next to her on the bench. Absently, Hope slipped her arm about the child's shoulders and pulled her close.

Betsy snuggled closer. "I'm sorry for making you mad earlier."

"Oh, honey. I'm sorry for hollering at you. I just don't want you catching your brother's sickness."

Betsy laid her cheek on Hope's shoulder. "You don't have to be afraid. Greg's not going to die."

"I hope you're right, Bets." She stroked the girl's braids. "All we can do is hope for the best."

"I dreamed he was real sick, but that he didn't die."

"When?" Hope pulled Betsy around to face her.

With wide, innocent eyes, the girl regarded her. "Right before I woke up."

"Today?" Hope's pulse picked up. If that were the case, Betsy would have had the dream before anyone knew Greg was ill.

"Yes. That's what I wanted to tell you. In my dream, you kept giving Greg lots and lots of water to drink. And after awhile he got better."

A shiver began at the base of Hope's spine and traveled quickly up her back. She shuddered and kissed Betsy hard on the head. "Thank you, sweetie!"

Hope shot to her feet and hurried to the wagon.

It seemed reasonable that if Greg was losing fluid from his body that he would need to replenish it. Thankfully, they'd camped near a creek for their noon stop. They could fill extra pots with water before they headed out. It might not stay cool, but it would replace the fluids he was losing. Was this another miracle brought about through the twins' faith? She hoped so, more than she'd ever hoped for anything in her life. When she reached the wagon, she threw open the flap.

"Andy. I know what we have to do."

๛

When Gregory emerged from the wagon weak, shaky, and pale, but alive nonetheless, the entire wagon train exploded in applause. Of all those who had come down ill, he alone survived.

In all, ten adults and fourteen children, including one newborn, had succumbed. Now, a week after Gregory's recovery, no new cases had been reported and cholera had finally run its course and moved on.

The pioneers breathed a collective sigh of relief. And for nearly a month, it appeared the face of God smiled on them.

The distant mountains loomed before them as a promise,

calling to the weary travelers, "Don't give up. Keep coming. It's been hard, but you've made it this far. Once you make the final climb, you'll enter your valley, your fields, your rivers and streams. Your promised land."

By early September, the breathtakingly beautiful mountains suddenly were no longer a distant goal, but a very real danger. As they ascended, jagged edges, slippery, snow-covered slopes, and near blizzard conditions made for slow going. Some days they traveled no more than a mile or two. But they pressed on, the air charged with determination. They hadn't come this far, lost stock, keepsakes, and for some, loved ones, only to fail. The trail down the mountain was even harder. Oxen and horses were walked down while wagons were lowered down by ropes.

Along with the change in scenery, Andy noticed a change in Hope. Serenity, reminiscent of his mother, radiated from her. When the children bowed their heads to say grace, she folded her hands and prayed along with them, not by way of humoring the twins, but in sincere thanks.

Gregory, too, seemed to have found comfort in faith since his close call. There was no denying the boy had changed. He worked willingly and swiftly. His face lit with an almost constant smile, as though he had a secret pleasure. Andy almost missed the incorrigible Gregory, the one who had made Andy feel as though Hope needed him. Now the boy was downright docile. Obedient. Good. And determined to become a preacher some day.

All this change made Andy uncomfortable. He hadn't counted on his new little family getting a dose of religion en route to their new home. Religious women made Andy nervous. Would Hope still be willing to keep to the bargain?

Now that home was only a couple of weeks away, Andy was having second thoughts about introducing Hope and the children to Ma.

Ma would take them into her heart before he finished the introductions. How could she help it? How could anyone not love the Parkers? *No, not the Parkers,* he reminded himself. They were his family. They were Rileys now.

"I was getting worried."

Hope's gentle voice broke through Andy's thoughts. He smiled. "Our worries are over now," he answered.

"Are they?"

Her tone held a serious note that he wasn't sure he could address just yet. There were too many questions floating through his own mind. Questions only he could answer. So he gave her a grin and pretended she meant physical worries. "Sure they are! We're safely over the mountains and in a few days, you and the children and I will veer away from the wagon train and head toward Hobbs, where my family lives.

"How long do you think it will take to file a claim and get our home built?"

"To tell you the truth, I have my own land already. I thought we'd build there."

"Oh, Andy, no. I can't take your land. You might want to build a. . .a home of your own, someday."

Her indomitable spirit gripped him. Andy observed her face, red from the sun and wind and cold. Now that they were on the other side of the mountains the weather was mild once more, but the harsh conditions had taken their toll on Hope. "If anyone deserves that land, it's you. I'd be pleased to give it to you and the children. I was never cut out to settle on a farm."

She lowered her gaze, but not before Andy noticed the disappointment flash across her face.

"Hope. . ."

Looking him full in the eye once more, she nodded. "It's all right. We had a bargain. And you have kept yours so far. I won't try to hold you past winter."

"But what about spring planting and harvest?" Andy's brow furrowed.

"You were right, Andy. I asked much more of you than you received payment for." She smiled and shame filled Andy as he remembered the night he'd tried to share her bed. She didn't dwell on that subject, but moved on. "Between Greg and me and perhaps a hired hand or two, we should be fine." She gave him a self-mocking smile. "If worse comes to worst, we wouldn't absolutely have to farm. I have plenty of money to last us. And my investments in Chicago are more than secure."

"Then why even bother? It's a rigorous life."

A shrug lifted her shoulders. "The Bible says hard work builds character. Or something like that."

"You have more character than anyone I know." The compliment flew from Andy's lips before he knew it was coming.

"Thank you, Andy. That means so much to me to hear you say that." She smiled and touched his arm. "But I am thinking more of my children. In the city, Greg got into trouble because he didn't have enough to occupy him. Coming to Oregon won't do anyone any good if I repeat the same mistakes I made in the first place."

"Greg's not the same boy he was when you left Chicago."

"Thanks be to God."

"Yeah," Andy muttered.

"And thanks to you, too. You taught him so much."

And it had been his pleasure. The boy was his one accomplishment, except now Hope was giving God the credit for the lad's change in behavior.

"Well, Lucille says supper is going to be ready in just a few minutes. That's the main reason I came looking for you." She turned to walk back to the circle of wagons then swung back to face him. "And Andy. If you meant it about the land, I'd be proud to build my home on your land. I just need to know. . ."

Andy tensed, afraid the question might be whether or not

he intended to share in their life from time to time. The question frightened him, because where he'd once known for certain that he had no intention of returning once he left, now he wasn't so sure. "What do you need to know?"

"I just. . . Well, do you want me to pay you for the land?"

Outrage filled Andy's chest and he scowled deeply. "Of course not. You're my family!"

A gasp escaped her lips before he realized what he'd implied.

"A–all right, Andy. Thank you, then. We accept your kindness."

She spun around and hurried away, leaving Andy to wonder why on earth he'd blurted such a fool thing. How had this gone from a business arrangement to the desire to provide for this family? His family.

He kicked a rock across the ground and headed in the direction Hope had taken. For the first time, he began to see the seriousness of bringing home a family to meet Ma and his brothers. They wouldn't understand the bargain. They wouldn't understand when he rode away.

Andy clenched his fist. They would be disappointed. But they didn't know the loss he'd endured. A loss so devastating, there was no way he could risk that again.

He had to keep his heart in check. To love as deeply as he'd loved Yellow Bird and his tiny daughter had nearly destroyed him. Never again. He pushed aside the longing and gathered a long, full breath in order to strengthen his resolve. Never, ever again.

eleven

The children's excitement was palpable as the town of Hobbs came into view. Hope's anticipation matched theirs, but anxiety slowly replaced her eagerness as she observed the neatly put-together townswomen walking along the boardwalks.

For the first time in months, Hope wondered about her appearance. Her mirror had long since broken, but she could only guess what a spectacle she made. How on earth could she possibly meet Andy's family in this condition?

"What's wrong?" Andy placed his hand on her arm.

"Oh, nothing."

It never failed to amaze Hope how intuitive Andy could be at times. A wave of sadness washed over her. He had the potential to be a wonderful husband. But she'd resigned herself to the situation.

Andy took both reins in one hand and slipped his other arm around her. "Something's wrong. If it's about my family, you have no reason to worry."

He released a shaky laugh, and Hope realized for the first time that he was nervous about seeing them again. "Believe me, they'll love you and the children. I'm the one who's likely to get a thrashing from one or both of my brothers and a sharp tongue lashing from my ma, and possibly my niece, since I didn't bring her another Indian doll."

"Well, you deserve it for not coming home in five whole years."

With a chuckle, Andy gave her an affectionate, one-armed hug and returned the reins to both hands.

Hope released a heavy sigh. "I just feel so. . ." Loathe to whine about something as trivial as the need for a bath and a new dress, Hope left the sentence open and averted her gaze to the dusty street.

"I understand."

In a few moments, the wagon pulled in front of a large two-story home. Andy hopped down and reached for Hope.

"I thought your family lived on a farm."

"They do. It won't hurt us to take an extra day to bathe and sleep in real beds before we go out to the farm."

Tears of relief stung Hope's eyes. "Do you think there are enough rooms available?"

"Only one way to find out." He winked and strode up to the front door. A few moments later, the dowager who came to the door had agreed to rent them two rooms for the night. Baths and supper cost extra. But Hope gladly paid for them all.

Francis had chosen to hook up with a small train headed to California and was no longer with the little family, so Gregory and Billy shared a room; Hope, Lucille, and Betsy occupied the other. Andy declined the invitation to share the boys' room.

"Where will you sleep?" Hope asked after he'd carried in her necessities for the night.

"I figure I'll look up my brother, Hank, and bed down at his place. Unless you think the parsonage might cave in if such a sinner slept in one of its rooms."

"Don't be silly." She smiled fondly at him. "Thank you for being so thoughtful, Andy. I'm looking forward to being clean."

He nodded. "Will you be all right for the rest of the day and evening? Or should I come back and take you to supper? There's a restaurant down the street."

Hope wished he had come out and said he'd be back to take her to supper. She would have loved the opportunity to share their supper together in Andy's hometown. But he apparently had other things on his mind.

"We'll be fine. I imagine we will take our supper here at the boardinghouse."

The process of bathing was a slow one. Water had to be heated and tossed out after each bath because the grime was so thick.

Mrs. Barker, the woman who owned the boardinghouse, obviously begrudged them every single bucketful, though she did seem pleased with their ability to pay for each bath.

By midafternoon, they were all clean and infinitely more comfortable than they'd been in months. When a knock sounded on the door, Hope assumed it was Mrs. Barker announcing supper, but a lovely woman stood there. She smiled, her green eyes twinkling in merriment. Several garments were slung over her arms.

"Hello. You must be Hope."

"Why, y—yes, I am." Clearly the woman had been sent. "What can I do for you?"

"My name's Rosemary. I'm a friend of Andy Riley's brother, Hank. Andy mentioned you might be needing some gowns. I just happen to own a dress shop. Isn't that a happy coincidence?" She gave a merry laugh.

Hope smiled. "It's wonderful."

The woman's friendly smile widened. "May I come in?"

"Please do." Hope opened the door further.

"Thank you." She walked to the bed and dumped the entire armload.

"I'm afraid I don't have anything for a child," she said, giving Betsy a worried frown.

Betsy's face drooped. "That's okay, ma'am," she murmured.

Hope smiled. "May I procure your services, Miss Rosemary? We all need new clothes."

"Yes, you may. It just so happens that I am fresh out of orders for now."

"Ma. . ."

At the sound of Billy's dread-filled voice, Hope smiled.

"Run along and find your brother." Relief washed his features.

Hope and Rosemary exchanged grins. It didn't take much to figure out the boy had dreaded the thought of being forced to stay in the room.

After he disappeared through the door, closing it behind him with a loud bang, Hope turned to Rosemary. "Maybe you can take Betsy's measurements while you're here and make her the first dress. Let's see, we'll need at least two serviceable gowns for Lucille and myself. And a couple of Sunday dresses each. W—will that be enough, do you think?"

The woman flashed a dimple, and Hope had a momentary spark of longing. Why couldn't she be beautiful like other women? Would Andy think Rosemary was lovely?

If he did, who could blame him?

The woman gave her an innocent, wide-eyed look and such a genuine smile, Hope felt foolish for her jealousy.

"I think five each will be plenty. Would you like to take a look at the gowns on the bed? You might find something to your liking among them." Rosemary rummaged through the gowns on the bed until she found the one she'd apparently been looking for, as evidenced by her smile of satisfaction. She gathered it by the shoulder fabric and held it up. "Oh, yes. Dark blue is going to look lovely on you."

Hope gave the gown a dubious look and sighed. Nothing was going to look "lovely" on her. The most she could hope for was passable.

"You don't like it?" Rosemary's disappointed tone captured Hope's attention from her maudlin thoughts. Hope nodded.

"Of course. I'm sorry. It's a beautiful gown. Do you think it's going to be long enough for me? I am rarely able to buy ready-made dresses without alterations."

Rosemary sized her up. "Hmmm, you're rather tall, aren't you? But that shouldn't be a problem if you leave off a hoop."

Hope laughed. "I haven't worn a hoop in five months. I'm not sure I even remember how to sit in one."

"You'll find the women around here are typically very practical. They dress in a proper manner, but practicality is much more important than fashion. It just so happens, this gown was ordered by a young bride-to-be whose engagement was called off at the last minute. The young woman held out the blue gown. "How about if you try this on while I start measuring Miss Betsy, here?" She winked at the little girl, eliciting a bright grin.

Hope took the gown and moved behind a privacy screen situated in the corner of the room.

"Do you and Andy plan to farm close to Michael and Star?" Rosemary asked, as she pulled out a tape measure and began taking measurements.

Hope felt her cheeks warm. She'd been anticipating the first questions about their plans, but thought she'd have another day at least. Neither she nor Andy had brought up the subject of how they would explain their arrangement. "We, uh, Andy mentioned building on land he has already. I assume it's close to his brother. I am looking forward to learning how to farm."

That seemed to satisfy the seamstress. She smiled. "Let's start with this one. I may have to take it up a bit."

For the next hour, the women concentrated on tacking the gowns where they were a bit big on both Lucille and Hope.

Each of the weary women came away with two dresses, despite Lucille's protest that Hope should keep all four. But

Hope wouldn't dream of it. Lucille had been worth her weight in gold. Hope planned to put her up in the boarding-house until Andy finished building their home, then Lucille would come to cook for them.

After the fittings and Rosemary's expert sewing skills took care of the mildly ill-fitting gowns, they ate a delicious meal of roasted chicken, potatoes, and carrots. Fresh bread topped the list of foods they'd done without for months. But best of all, Mrs. Barker had baked a fresh apple pie.

No one wanted the meal to end. When every morsel was cleaned from the table, Mrs. Barker finally proclaimed her kitchen officially closed. She seemed gruff, but Hope could tell the woman relished the compliments and declarations of pure joy at the fare she'd set before her flavor-starved boarders.

By the time Hope settled into bed that night, Betsy beside her and Lucille on a cot, her mind whirled with the events of the day. Rolling into Hobbs with Andy at her side, a real bath, new clothes, a wonderful supper, and now a soft bed. She smiled into the darkness. She wasn't sure she'd want to get out of bed in the morning. But she knew she'd have to. Andy was anxious to see his ma.

Tension suddenly clutched her stomach as she remembered that tomorrow she'd be meeting her mother-in-law for the first time. What would the woman think when she learned the nature of her relationship with her son?

Squeezing her eyes tightly, she tried in vain to force herself to drift to sleep, but despite the feather bed, she couldn't still her mind. So much had changed since they'd set out on their journey last spring. So much. She'd changed. For one thing, she believed in God now.

How could she not after all the miracles He'd performed during the journey? And not just for her and her children. She'd seen the pioneers beat the odds over and over and, more often than not, the results could only be attributed to something greater than human effort.

Andy's unwitting prophecy concerning Gregory had come to pass. The boy had changed so much that Hope barely recognized the same child. Not only had he grown physically, he had truly changed. Where it counted the most. In his heart.

Grateful tears slipped from her eyes and wet the hair at her temples. Every hardship had been worth it for this end result.

She tried not to think about what would happen once winter ended and Andy left. Sometimes she could kick herself for giving him that early out. Why hadn't she hung on for the full year? Every moment with him was that much longer that he might, just might, fall in love with her and decide to stay with them forever.

Flopping over onto her stomach, she breathed out a frustrated sigh. If she didn't stop thinking foolish thoughts that would never, ever come true and get some sleep, she'd meet Andy's family with bags under her eyes and look even more hideous than ever.

Listening to Betsy's even breathing lulled Hope to a state of relaxation, and the last thing she wondered before she drifted to sleep was whether or not Andy was ashamed to introduce her as his bride. Was that why he'd left her at a boardinghouse while he went to his brother's home?

&

Andy could feel Hope's apprehension, and it was starting to make him nervous. Hank had sent word to Ma and Michael and Star last night that Andy was home and would be bringing his new family out today. He hadn't had the heart to tell Hank the truth of the matter—that Hope had essentially hired him to be her husband and would set him free, if not legally, then certainly morally.

Andy already knew that his mother would be mortified,

Hank disapproving, and Michael downright disgusted at the arrangement. For the first time, he wondered if perhaps they shouldn't tell the family. Hope was going to have enough adjusting to do without bearing the brunt of family speculation.

"Hope. I have an idea."

"Oh?" Hope turned to him, her silky eyebrows lifted. Her blue eyes were twice as vibrant as usual. Andy had to admit she looked quite attractive in her new blue gown and bonnet.

Forcing his mind back to the topic at hand, he leaned in a little closer so the children who sat in the back wouldn't overhear them. The day before he had removed the canvas and had replaced the nearly dead oxen with a pair of fresh horses. He figured they made quite a domestic picture. Ma, Pa, and youngsters all going to Grandma's house. The picture excited him and disturbed him all at once.

"What is it, Andy?"

"Look. I don't want my family asking a lot of questions. I. . . what do you think of just keeping our arrangement between the two of us?"

"They're going to find out sooner or later anyway."

He scowled. "Better later than sooner as far as I'm concerned."

"I won't lie to keep you from being uncomfortable. But as long as no one asks me, I won't volunteer the information."

A smile tipped his lips. He reached out and covered her hand. "Thank you."

Andy's heart leapt at the first sight of Ma standing outside the log cabin home. Andy appraised the cabin. It appeared Michael had added a room since Andy had been here last. He wondered what reception he'd get from his sister-in-law, Star. He'd insulted her when he'd last visited home. As a matter of fact, his words had caused a scuffle with Michael. Andy had left the next day. According to Hank, Michael and Star had married that winter. The following year, Star had borne Michael a son. She now carried their second child.

The news had caused Andy a restless night, dreaming about Yellow Bird and their child. Would he ever be free?

Feeling Hope tense beside him, he came back to the present. And to his ma's beaming face. He stepped down and before he knew it, Ma was in his arms, weeping for what Andy hoped was joy.

"It's so good to see you, son." Her words were muffled against his shoulder and he could feel her plump body shudder with sobs.

She pulled away. Andy produced a handkerchief and pressed it into her hand. She wiped at her eyes and nose then grasped each of his upper arms. "Let me look at you." Andy squirmed a bit under her scrutiny. Her brow furrowed in worry.

There were more lines in her face than he remembered, and he couldn't help but wonder with more than a little guilt if he was the cause.

"Are you going to introduce me to your new family?"

"Huh? Oh! Of course." Heat seared Andy's ears. He turned to the wagon where Hope still sat. Shame slithered through him. He should have helped her down before he even embraced his ma.

"I'm sorry," he whispered, pulling her a little closer than necessary. Her eyes lit with surprised as she looked up at him.

"It's all right, Andy. I didn't mind."

He took her hand and led her to his mother. "Ma, this is Hope, my. . .uh. . .wife."

Tears sprang once more into Ma's eyes. She stood between Andy and Hope and looked between them. "I just knew when you found the right woman you'd finally come home." Hope seemed stunned to find herself suddenly cradled in Ma's embrace. Her eyes grew wide as she looked at Andy over Ma's shoulder.

Andy grinned. That was his ma. A mother to all.

"Can we get down now, Ma?"

Billy's impatient voice broke the emotional moment, and Ma pulled away with a laugh. "Yes, you may come over here and meet your new Grammy."

Predictably, the children and Ma formed an instant bond. Andy's chest swelled and he suddenly felt as though he truly had come home.

twelve

"I'm sorry? You want us to. . . ?" Hope nearly choked on a bite of venison roast as she stared across the table at her mother-in-law.

"Stay here while your house is built, of course." The lady looked back at her with brows furrowed. "Where else did you intend to stay?"

"I thought, well, I hadn't really thought about it. The boardinghouse, I suppose."

"And subject the children to Mrs. Barker's ridiculous rules? The woman allows bathing only on Saturdays. She won't abide talking loud enough for her to hear past seven o'clock because she retires early. Can your children whisper all evening? And if you are ten minutes late for breakfast, she refuses to serve you. Isn't that right, Star?"

Star Riley, Michael's wife, nodded, her beautiful violet-colored eyes sparkling in amusement. "That isn't the half of it. Believe me, you're better off staying here."

"Oh, but we couldn't put you out, could we, Andy?"

He'd been so busy shoveling food into his mouth, Hope doubted he'd heard a word his mother had said. If he had, he certainly didn't seem too concerned. Hope gave him a sound kick under the table.

By his pained expression, she realized she might have applied more force than necessary.

"What were you saying?" he asked, but Hope could tell by his too-innocent expression that he knew exactly what they were saying. Her temper flared at his cowardice. He just thought he'd weasel his way out of having to confront it like a man. Why did even the manliest of men turn into a sniveling child when it meant standing up to his ma?

"Your mother invited us to stay here while the house is being built."

"Yes," Mrs. Riley said in a definitive tone. "It's much more convenient. Besides the practical matter of saving money on the boardinghouse, you will only be a couple of miles from the building site. It's not reasonable to go back and forth to town each day."

Andy caught Hope's attention, clearly won over by his mother's logic. Glowering, Hope gave him another kick.

He grimaced. "Really, we couldn't put you folks out. We don't mind staying at the boardinghouse for a couple of weeks."

"Nonsense," Michael spoke up. "With the new room we added last spring, we're floating in extra space. It would be an insult for you to pay for a place to sleep when you can stay here. Betsy can bunk with Aimee, the two boys can have the loft, and you and Hope can share our old room. It's just sitting empty now waiting for the new baby.

Hope inwardly groaned at the word "insult." Given Miss Hannah's logic and Michael's use of the guilt-inducing word, there was no way they could justify not accepting the offered hospitality.

She gave a helpless shrug and Andy smiled—a mildly triumphant smile. "I suppose we'll have to accept. Thank you for your kind offer."

"Thank goodness, that's settled." Miss Hannah bit into a slice of bread, capturing Hope's gaze. She stared for just a flash too long. Before she looked away, Hope saw concern in the older woman's eyes. Alarm seized Hope. If Andy's mother were that astute, there would be no keeping their secret, not if they were living under the same roof.

◈

A heavy knot formed in Hope's stomach as she changed into her nightgown in the darkness. True, Andy wasn't in the room, but that didn't mean he couldn't walk in any second. After she'd excused herself for the night, she'd heard him ask Michael to show him a colt that had been born during the spring.

Hope had a fleeting suspicion that he might have done so in order to give her a little privacy. But she gave a short laugh at the notion. If Andy were truly noble, he'd have just come right out with the truth, no matter what the consequences.

But that wasn't really fair either, because she wasn't crazy about the idea of the family knowing the truth herself. They knew what was most important for them to know, that she was married to Andy in a legal and binding manner. There would be no annulment. But Andy would walk away when he was ready and that would be that. She would be left to explain it to his family and the twins.

Her temper flared at the thought. How dare he just leave her to do the dirty work! To pick up the pieces of her children's broken hearts.

By the time she heard Andy's footsteps walk down the hall and stop at their door, Hope had worked herself into a full-blown mad. She turned her back and pretended to be asleep just as he stepped inside.

The other side of the mattress sank beneath his weight as he sat and started to remove his boots. Her pulse pounded in her ears. When he stretched out, she couldn't take it another second. In one swift movement, she flopped over to face him.

"What do you think you are doing?" she demanded.

Andy let out a yowl and shot from the bed, clad in his long handles. "Woman, you scared me half to death!"

Averting her gaze, although it wasn't necessary in the darkened room, Hope hissed, "Keep your voice down, you imbecile.

Or do you want your whole family to come running?"

"Why were you pretending to be asleep?"

"Because I didn't want to talk to you."

"What changed your mind?"

"I realized you thought you'd actually sleep in the bed with me."

"Where else?" Andy sat on the bed once more.

"On the floor, of course. We brought plenty of quilts so that you can make it nice and comfy. You are not sleeping in this bed with me."

"I'm not sleeping on the floor after five months on the ground. You have my word that I won't come near you."

"That's not good enough." Hope sat up, covers to her chin. "I insist that you sleep on the floor."

Andy gave her a stubborn scowl and leaned in so close Hope could feel his breath on her cheek. "If my word isn't good enough, then I guess you'll have to sleep on the floor yourself."

He stretched out and closed his eyes.

A gasp escaped Hope's throat at his utter lack of chivalry. She jumped out of bed. "Fine, Andy Riley, I'll make a pallet and sleep on it myself."

She made herself a thick pallet and stretched out. Andy sat up on his elbow and watched her. "Why won't you just sleep up here? My promise is good."

"Your promise has nothing to do with it. I believe you. It's my promise to myself that I care about."

"What sort of promise?"

"That I wouldn't share my bed with another man who doesn't love me."

Andy remained silent for a moment, then he swung his legs over the side of the bed and rested his elbows on his knees. "You win. I'll take the floor."

"Never mind. I'm down here now. I might as well stay."

"Get in the bed, Hope."

"No."

A low growl emanated from his throat. Before she knew what was happening, Hope felt herself being lifted from the floor.

She kicked her feet in protest, but it did no good. He stomped to the bed and gave her a toss.

"When I say I'm sleeping on the floor, that's exactly what I mean." His chest heaved and he glowered at her. The sight of him leaning over her sent Hope's heart into a tizzy.

"Hope. . ."

Some day she'd learn not to be so transparent. "Forget it, Andy. Business arrangement only."

"Fine by me." His hard tone gave a hint at his wounded pride, and Hope wished things could be different. But she had to protect her heart. At most, she had six months with Andy. It was going to be difficult enough to let him go without falling into a real relationship with him. She gave a deep sigh. From the pallet, she heard Andy do the same.

≈

"Whoa, take it easy, Andy." Hank gave him a good-natured clap on the shoulder. "You're going to clean out these woods in one day at the pace you're going. I can't keep up."

Andy straightened up and sank the ax head into the stump of tree he'd just felled. He accepted the proffered canteen and gratefully took in several gulps of water.

"Thanks."

"So do you want to tell me what's bothering you?"

Andy gave a short laugh. "Don't start pulling that preacher stuff on me."

A flash of hurt appeared in Hank's eyes, and Andy immediately regretted his rash comment.

"Hey, I was teasing. Nothing's wrong. I just want to get Hope's house built as soon as possible. The sooner she's settled in her own home, the better."

"Is there a problem at Michael's?"

Other than the fact that I'm sleeping on the floor every night, gritting my teeth to keep from climbing into bed with my wife and taking her into my arms?

Of course he kept the thought to himself. He shrugged. "You know a woman wants her own kitchen."

"I thought Hope hired a cook."

"Well, yeah. Hope doesn't want her own kitchen." Andy scowled, knowing he'd been caught in his fib. "That's just a figure of speech anyway."

"I see." Hank straddled the newly downed tree and regarded Andy with eyes that seemed to capture the essence of his soul. Shifting uncomfortably, Andy averted his gaze.

"Is everything all right with your marriage, Andy?" Hank's voice sang with genuine caring, and as much as Andy would have liked to suggest his brother mind his own business, he couldn't. So he lied instead.

"Everything's fine." He forced a grin. "Hope's quite a woman. Just the kind of spitfire an old grizzly bear like me needs to keep me on the straight and narrow."

"Are you on the straight and narrow, Andy?"

Andy gave himself a swift inward kick. Why had he used such idiotic words when talking to a preacher?

"Now, Hank. I told you not to start that preacher stuff with me."

"Whether I was a preacher or not, I'd still be concerned for your soul."

"Don't be."

"So you're telling me you're doing fine with God? Or are you telling me to butt out of your affairs?"

"Little brother, God forgot about me a long time ago." He felt a twinge of unease. He couldn't deny God's help in retrieving Hope from the Indians.

" 'Whither shall I go from thy spirit? or whither shall I flee from thy presence?' "

The hair on the back of Andy's neck rose at the sound of Hank's voice.

" 'If I ascend up into heaven, thou art there: if I make my bed in hell, behold, thou art there. If I take the wings of the morning, and dwell in the uttermost parts of the sea; even there shall thy hand lead me, and thy right hand shall hold me. If I say, Surely the darkness shall cover me; even the night shall be light about me. Yea, the darkness hideth not from thee; but the night shineth as the day: the darkness and the light are both alike to thee.' "

Silence saturated the air between them, like a fat cloud about to burst with rain.

"You don't know where I've been for five years, Hank. If you knew, you wouldn't be so all-fired sure that God of yours was looking out for me."

"Tell me where you've been."

Heaving a troubled sigh, Andy shook his head. "Some things are better left alone."

"Anything hidden will eventually be brought into the light, Andy. One way or another."

"I suppose you pulled that from the Bible, too?"

"Yes."

Andy nodded. "Well, I guess break time is about over. Those logs aren't going to pull themselves to the building site."

"Looks like we're in for a storm."

Andy followed his gaze to the sky, suddenly dark with storm clouds.

Hank tossed the canteen into the back of the wagon. "Maybe

we'd best head on back to the house. It's about supper time anyway and you know what Ma said."

A grin tipped Andy's lips. "We'd best not be late or we'll be eating with the pigs."

"Ma's a character." Hank chuckled as they began loading the axes and saws into the wagon. "You know, she's beside herself that all her sons are settled down close to her."

"I reckon she is." Andy swallowed hard and climbed into the wagon. He took up the reins and waited until Hank was seated before nudging the horses toward home.

"She's taken quite a liking to Hope and the children."

"Yep." Why couldn't he just be quiet about it? Andy's stomach churned. Hank's fresh optimism had always been a source of irritation for Andy and no less now.

"The boy, Gregory, seems to be a good lad." Something in Hank's tone raised Andy's suspicion. He cut a glance toward Hank.

"He is."

"He came to me a couple of days ago and told me he'd like to become a preacher. Asked me for some advice. What do you think of that?"

Andy shrugged. "The boy has a right to do whatever he wants. I guess you didn't turn out too bad. Any advice you give him couldn't hurt." He sent his brother a sardonic grin. "What help would I be to a boy hankering to be a preacher?"

"There's more, actually, that I should probably just come right out and tell you."

Swallowing past the sudden lump in his throat, Andy stared straight ahead. Focused on Hank's forthcoming revelation, he didn't flinch when a flash of lightning streaked across the sky.

Hank cleared his throat. "The truth is, Gregory's concerned about your relationship with his ma."

Andy scowled. This was the last conversation he wanted to have. Irritation shot through him at the boy, but he supposed he couldn't really blame Gregory, not after what he'd seen and overheard that night by the creek. But did the boy have to go telling all their secrets? True, they'd never actually told him not to go blabbing their relationship to people, but some things should be a simple matter of common sense.

"Do you have anything to say to what I just told you?" Hank's voice seemed a little irritated, and Andy's defenses rose.

Unsure what Gregory had revealed, he decided to keep his comments nonspecific rather than give Hank more information than he needed.

"Well, I guess it's natural for a boy to worry about his ma's new man. But don't concern yourself, we'll work it out."

Hank slapped his thigh in a rare show of frustration. "Listen to what I'm telling you, man. Your new son told me about your arrangement with Hope. I know you two don't have a real marriage, I know she's paying you to build her house, and I know you plan on leaving after a year."

The truth on Hank's lips made the whole thing suddenly seem like a bad idea. Andy could feel everything unraveling. He hated the thought of what his ma would think once she discovered what a cad he was. Andy glared at his brother. "All right. So now that you know, what do you plan to do about it?"

thirteen

Hope had sensed Andy's foul mood all evening. His stormy expression matched the storm outside. She only hoped he didn't start thundering.

The tension inside the cabin was so thick, Betsy and Aimee had excused themselves to their room. The two girls were close enough in age, with Aimee being only three years older, that they'd formed a fast bond. It did Hope's heart good to see her daughter with her first true girlfriend ever. But she couldn't help but feel a little sorry for Billy. He hadn't been prepared for his sister's defection, and he had been moping for days. Next week, she intended to send the children to town school, so she prayed Billy would find a friend.

Miss Hannah sat in her wooden chair and rocked before the fire, her knitting needles clacking against each other, moving so fast it made Hope dizzy to watch her. Star, too, sat with knitting in hand. Thanks to these two women's efforts, Star's baby would be well outfitted.

Michael sat at the table going over the accounts of the farm and looking mighty pleased with himself, from what Hope could tell.

Only Andy seemed out of sorts. He paced, sat, paced, sat, and paced some more until Hope could stand it no longer. She jumped up, announced bedtime to Billy and Gregory, and bade everyone good night.

Inside her bedroom, she quickly donned her nightgown, spread Andy's pallet for him—figuring that was the least she could do—and slid beneath the covers. She'd barely closed her eyes when she heard Andy's heavy boots.

Without making his usual attempt at courtesy by trying to be quiet, he got ready for bed. Alarm seized her when she felt him lift the covers and slide in beside her.

With a gasp, she sat up pulling the covers to her chin. "What do you think you're doing?"

He gave a snort. "So, you're not really asleep. I don't know why you always pretend to be asleep when I come into the room. I told you I wouldn't bother you."

"Whether I'm asleep or not is none of your business," she snapped. "What are you doing in the bed? I. . .I fixed your pallet for you."

"How sweet."

His sarcasm was beginning to grate on her good nature. But she bit back a hostile comment, afraid it might make him more determined to be stubborn.

"Andy," she said through her gritted teeth. "We had an arrangement."

Her heart nearly stopped as he sat up. The starless night allowed for no light to shine in the room, still she could see the hard lines of his face, determined. He slid his hand behind her neck, lacing his fingers through her hair. In a swift movement, he brought her face close. "Maybe I'm tired of the arrangement."

"Y—you can't just get tired of it." Barely able to emit a sound through her closed throat, Hope wasn't sure he'd heard her. He pressed kisses over her cheeks, eyelids, and forehead.

"Andy, please." She despised the trembling in her voice.

Oh, how she wished she could share her life and her love with this man. But how could she give him the most precious gift she had to offer when he would be leaving in a matter of months?

"You promised," she whispered.

"Promises are made to be broken," he said, his voice filled with husky emotion.

Hope steeled her heart, knowing if she didn't put a stop to this immediately, his lips would find hers and she would be lost.

In a beat, she maneuvered away. His face came down on her shoulder.

"Hey," he growled.

"W—we had an agreement." Gathering the blanket close, she swallowed back tears. "I thought you were an honorable man."

He gave a short laugh and flung himself back on the bed. "I don't know what ever gave you that idea. When you met me I was about to be killed for gambling away another man's money. Not much honor in that is there?"

Unable to bear his mocking tone, she took his self-deprecation as a personal affront. "Don't you dare belittle yourself, Andy Riley. I don't know what drove you to drinking and gambling, I can only guess you were in love and lost her."

He drew in a swift breath of air. "Why do you say that?"

"You called me Yellow Bird that first day when you were so badly injured."

All the fight seemed to leave him. "She was my wife."

Hope's outrage melted away, and Hope lay on her side, her ear pressing into her palm as she rose on her elbow. "Do you want to talk about it?"

"She was the most beautiful thing I'd ever seen. I fell in love with her from the first moment I laid my eyes on her."

Hope's stomach sank at the longing in his tone, and she wished she hadn't opened the door for him to confide his grief. He seemed to have forgotten she was there anyway as he spoke into the darkness.

"Yellow Bird was the first woman I ever loved. I spent my youth scouting for wagon trains, carousing when I could, and generally spending time with women who weren't looking for a man to settle down and make honest women of them."

Uninterested in hearing about his association with those kinds of women, Hope swallowed and pressed, "And how did you meet Yellow Bird?"

"I was hunting away from the wagon train one day, and something spooked my horse. I'm not sure what it was. Yellow Bird always believed it was The Great Spirit who did what was necessary so we could meet." He gave an affectionate laugh.

Jealousy twisted Hope's gut. This unknown woman still had Andy's heart. Her husband's heart. The pain of it nearly took her breath. But she pushed it aside. "Go on."

"I was thrown from my horse and knocked unconscious. My first memory when I woke up in a Sioux village was Yellow Bird's face leaning over me, her black hair loose and brushing against my face. It took me minutes to realize she wasn't a dream."

His voice faded as he became lost in thought. Hope waited in the silence until he remembered she was there and continued.

"I stayed longer than I needed to. And soon I decided not to leave at all. The Sioux often adopt captives into the tribe and even though I wasn't technically a prisoner, I became one of the tribe. Those were the happiest days of my life. In a few months, I had enough ponies to offer Yellow Bird's father an extravagant bride price. He accepted, and Yellow Bird became my wife. She was with child very soon." His voice choked.

Sensing that this was the first time he'd ever opened up about this, Hope pushed aside her own hurt that she was competing with a dead woman for his affection. She wasn't sure she'd ever win his heart, but for certain, Andy would never love her until he was free of Yellow Bird's memory.

She reached out and placed her hand on his arm. He grabbed it as though taking hold of a life preserver. She winced as he clung to her.

"Yellow Bird was so happy to be carrying our child. She knew in her heart that she carried a girl. We haggled over names. I teased her by calling the baby Becky and Mary and Elizabeth. But she insisted there was no meaning in such common white names. And that we would decide what to call her after we knew her."

He gathered a ragged breath and gripped Hope's hand tighter. "But we never got to know her. A few months into the pregnancy, Yellow Bird started to bleed. It happened so fast. One minute she was grinning and sitting on my lap, tickling my chin. The next she was doubled over and three hours later she was dead. And so was our tiny baby girl. Sh—she was barely the size of my hand."

Tears thickened Hope's throat. She swallowed hard. "Oh, Andy. I'm so sorry."

"Her family wanted me to stay in the village. But I couldn't. Everything reminded me of her. The only way I could get relief was from a bottle. And that's what I did. I gambled and drank. I'd borrow money to gamble, and then made back more than I borrowed. Until my luck ran out a couple of years ago.

"The way you found me in the alley—that's the way I'd been living for two years. I've been beat up more times than I can count for owing money. I thought this time my luck had finally run out for good. I was ready to be put out of my misery. I wanted to join my wife and daughter, wherever they were. But you saved me and here we are."

Hope wasn't sure how to respond. She recalled his misery when he'd discovered he wasn't dead. Ridiculously, she almost felt as though she should apologize for saving him. But of course, she didn't. "Thank you for sharing that with me, Andy. I'm honored you trusted me with it."

"Thank you for listening." He slid his thumb over the back of her hand. "I'm sorry I tried to take liberties. I'll get down on the floor."

"Wait a little while, Andy. It makes a lot more sense for you to lie up here while we talk. I. . .I was hoping you'd tell me about the plans for the house. How are things coming along?"

Her eyes had adjusted to the dark room and she made out his smile.

"We cut down several trees today. Hank and Michael think we can start building next week. We hope to get a couple of main rooms up and a roof before the first real winter storm hits."

They discussed the building plans until long into the night. Finally, during a lull in the conversation, Andy's snoring alerted her to the fact that he'd fallen asleep. Hope was about to ease out of bed when the door opened. Betsy slipped inside. "Are you awake, Ma?"

Alarm shot through Hope. What would the little girl think of seeing Andy in her bed? Heat seared her cheeks. But there was nothing she could do about it now.

"I'm over here, Bets. What's wrong?"

"I have to tell you something."

"Okay. Keep your voice down so you don't wake Andy."

The child nodded, but didn't seem to notice one way or another where Andy was sleeping. Hope marveled. Things were so simple for children. Married people shared a bed and that was that. They didn't think beyond the obvious.

Betsy knelt beside Hope's bed. Hope turned onto her side, much as she had when listening to Andy, and once again rested her head on her palm. "Tell me what's bothering you."

"Do you know about Jesus, Ma?"

"You mean in the Bible?"

Betsy nodded.

"I suppose I do, honey. You know I've been believing in God ever since he made Gregory all well."

The little girl shook her head impatiently, almost frantically. "It's not enough just to believe in God. You have to believe that Jesus is His Son."

"Where did you hear that, honey?"

Hope had a rudimentary knowledge of religious beliefs from her association with the wagon train folks. But throughout her growing-up years, her father had seen to it that her primary playmates were children of intellectuals who, at best, believed only in the existence of a powerful being. Religion was scoffed at, Jesus considered a myth. Hope intended to procure a copy of the Bible at the earliest opportunity so that she might study it for herself.

"Are you listening, Ma?"

Betsy's voice snapped her back to the present. "I'm sorry, baby. Yes, I'm here."

"Aimee told me tonight all about Jesus." Tears quivered in Betsy's voice. "Ma, He *died* because I'm a sinner."

Taking Betsy's hand, Hope looked the girl square in the eye. "Sweetheart, you are not a sinner. You're a sweet little girl." Anger flared at Aimee, though the child was obviously twisting something she'd been taught. Parents should be more careful what they said in front of their children.

"Ma, we are *all* sinners. That's why Jesus had to die."

"Sweetie, I know Aimee believes that, but sinners are people that steal or kill people. Not folks like us and certainly not little girls like you." She smiled and smoothed Betsy's hair away from her face. "Does that make you feel better?"

The little girl flung Hope's hand away and stood. "Ma!"

"Shh, Betsy, come back here and keep your voice down.

Do you want to wake Andy?"

Betsy obeyed. "Ma, you have to listen to me. The Bible says we are *all* sinners. Only the blood of Jesus can wash us clean."

"Oh, Betsy, really, blood? What have you two girls been talking about?"

"Mama, please." Tears flowed in earnest now, and Betsy took Hope's hand in both of her little ones. "Please listen to me."

"All right, sweetheart." Hope made a mental note to clear this whole thing up with Miss Hannah in the morning.

Betsy drew a shaky breath. "Aimee said only accepting what Jesus did on the cross could make us acceptable to go to heaven. Even if you're a good person, unless you understand the sacrifice God's only Son made then you aren't saved."

"I've never heard of such a thing, Bets."

"I know, but Ma, when she was talking, my heart started beating really fast. Like now. And I just couldn't stop crying, thinking about the nails hammered in Jesus' hands and feet."

"Oh, baby, don't think about it, if it makes you cry. It's just a story."

"No! Ma, it's the truth. You know how you can always tell when Billy and me is lying?"

"Yes. But that's—"

"I just knew that Aimee was telling me the truth. And then she read to me out of her Bible. All about how He healed people and I thought about Gregory. Jesus healed him, Mama. Jesus did it, and we didn't even know He died for us. He just healed Greg because we asked Him to."

The conviction in Betsy's voice couldn't be denied. The child was a believer through and through. But what if it was all a myth like Father had always maintained? What if Greg had simply beaten the illness on his own? The very thought felt disloyal.

She thought of her studies. What of Pascal's wager? The philosopher had argued against his opponents that believed there was no God. Pascal responded that it was better to go ahead and believe in God. Because if there was no God and you believed anyway, at the end of your life, there would be no repercussions for your disbelief. If, on the other hand, you didn't believe and discovered after you died that indeed there was a God all along, then you were damned for your disbelief.

Hope had taken that wager to heart as a young girl and had allowed herself a rudimentary faith in God. Though the strength of her belief had varied over the years. Now she was faced with something different. This wasn't a vague belief in a distant God, this was a gut-wrenching, life-altering conviction. Something she'd always sworn never to adhere to or allow in her children.

"Betsy. Don't you remember the reverend on the wagon train?"

"Yes."

"If this were true, don't you think he would have told you about Jesus?"

"I think he thought we knew. He used to mention Jesus and the cross, but I never understood what he meant. And I didn't want to make him feel bad by telling him I didn't know what he was talking about."

Releasing a heavy sigh, Hope felt compassion well up for her daughter. How young to be so conflicted. She was so glad her father had kept her away from religion until she was old enough to make up her own mind.

"Honey, I don't want you to listen to Aimee about this anymore, all right? Tomorrow we'll discuss it with Miss Hannah."

"I can't wait until tomorrow. I have to do it now."

Hope frowned. "Do what?"

"Pray to ask Jesus in my heart."

"Ask Jesus into your heart? What on earth does that mean?"

"Aimee said it means that you tell Him you believe who Jesus is and you tell Him you're sorry for all of your sins. And then you ask Him to wash you clean and you get to start all over with no sin."

Hope gave her daughter an indulgent smile. "That sounds a little like magic."

"Not magic, Mama. A miracle."

The hair on the back of Hope's neck stood up at the awe in her daughter's voice.

"I can't wait another minute to pray. But I had to come tell you about it, too. Will you pray with me?"

"Oh, Bets. I don't know what you want me to say."

"Just say you will."

Hope could not deny her daughter, but neither could she pretend to embrace this new idea of asking Jesus into one's heart. It sounded a little strange.

"Tell you what. I will bow my head just like I do before we eat, okay? And you pray whatever you want to pray."

"Oh, I wanted you to ask Jesus to come into your heart, too."

"I can't do that. This idea is too new to me. But I promise I will purchase a Bible soon, and I'll keep an open mind while I read it. Fair enough?"

Betsy gave a hesitant nod. "Promise you'll get one tomorrow?"

"I'll try. Are you ready to pray your prayer now?"

"Yes."

Betsy bowed her head. "Dear God. Aimee says I'm a sinner. And I know she's telling the truth because I felt it in my stomach when she said it. But she said you sent Jesus and He died on the cross so that I don't have to go to the place where bad people go." She dropped her voice to a whisper. "I'm not allowed to say the name of the place bad people go, and I didn't think You'd want me starting off by disobeying Ma."

Hope smiled through tears. She couldn't help herself. Betsy's simple, wholesome belief in what she was saying filled her with a sense of awe.

"I know I done a lot of bad things. There are so many I can't remember them, but Aimee said I don't have to list them, just have to ask You to forgive them. So that's what I'm doing. Please make me good. Jesus, I never knew until tonight that You died for me." Her voice cracked. "B—but now that I do, I. . .I have to thank you. I wish You were down here in person so I could hug You to show you how much I love You. But I know You feel it. Just like I do right now. I. . .I didn't ask You yet, but I think You live in my heart now because I feel different. Oh, thank You, Jesus. Amen."

Hope opened her eyes and stared at her daughter.

"Can you tell I'm different, Ma?"

"I. . .Well, Bets, not really."

"You will."

"How do you know you're different? What if it didn't take?"

"Aimee says we have to accept these things by faith. And that if we believe we're truly different, we'll start acting different."

"I think you're pretty sweet just the way you are, so don't act too differently, okay?"

Betsy giggled. "I have to go wake up Aimee and tell her."

"Don't you think you should wait until morning?"

"I can't."

The little girl jumped to her feet and tippy-toe ran to the door.

" 'Night, Ma."

" 'Night."

Hope lay back down, bewildered by what had just transpired.

Closing her eyes, she thought fleetingly that she should perhaps retire to the pallet, but her weary body refused to move.

She listened to the sound of distant thunder as the storm

finally moved away. A gentle rain still tapped the window, and the wind sifted through the branches outside.

As she sank into the first phase of sleep, she was almost certain she heard the wind whispering, *"Only believe."*

She wanted to open her eyes, to see if someone had spoken to her or if the wind outside had caused her ears to play tricks on her. But her eyes were too heavy. Finally, she surrendered to sleep.

Only believe.

fourteen

Andy stood inside the door of the home he'd built for Hope. His gaze took in the wooden rocker he'd crafted with his own hands, the table with two benches for the children and two chairs, one at each end. He'd worked on the furniture as a surprise. He'd built a bed frame for her, and with Ma's help, he'd stuffed a mattress.

Betsy, too, had a bed. The boys would sleep on pallets in the loft until he could build the other bed frames. Taking the time to make furniture had extended their stay at Michael's for two extra weeks, but Andy resisted the idea of bringing Hope to an empty house.

Lately, he could sense that she was getting antsy, and he had begun running out of excuses as to why she couldn't come see the cabin. And, though he still worked hard and took some satisfaction in knowing Hope would have her own home, the joy and anticipation he'd expected to feel were glaringly absent. And he knew why. It had all started a month ago. When Betsy had tiptoed into their bedroom and proclaimed herself a sinner.

The Bible says we are all sinners. Only the blood of Jesus can wash us clean.

For weeks, those words had haunted Andy. They pounded into his brain with every swing of the ax, every bang of the hammer. Every waking moment.

In his dreams, Jesus, His eyes filled with love and compassion, beckoned with nail-scarred hands. Andy's dreamlike self tried to reach Him, but always stopped short of touching the hands. If he could only reach Jesus, Andy knew his restlessness would be over.

But he always awoke, drenched in sweat and tears and feeling emptier than he'd ever felt in his life. More than empty, he felt lost.

He wished he'd never eavesdropped on the conversation between Hope and Betsy that night. Had Hope known he was awake, she would have taken Betsy in the other room so as not to disturb him. But he'd been mesmerized by the wonder of the girl's discovery of things Andy had known from childhood. He'd allowed his heart to cry out for peace and with the acknowledgement of that longing, his faith had resurfaced.

But believing in God again opened another door—the feeling that he didn't—nor could he ever—measure up. To deny the existence of a Holy God was to excuse his behavior, no matter how despicable. There was simply nothing to aspire to. As a youngster, he'd learned that was the easier road. The narrow road Ma had always talked about seemed too hard. Andy never could quite get it right.

Because of that failure, he had always felt like the outsider in his family. Michael was the responsible one. Hank, the holy one. Andy had found his place as the black sheep, the troublemaker, the one who broke his mother's heart.

"I think that about does it." The sound of Michael's voice pulled Andy from his brooding.

"I guess so."

"I reckon Hope will be glad to have her own home."

Andy gave him a sharp glance. "You mean you're ready for us to move on?"

A frown creased Michael's brow. "No, that's not what I said. I just imagine your wife is ready to set up housekeeping for herself. You know how women are."

Knowing he owed his brother an apology didn't sit well with Andy. He scowled. "You don't know Hope. She's not like most women. She's been a real trooper—on the trail and since we've been staying with you."

Michael gave a curt nod and gathered a breath. Andy could tell he was trying to keep his temper in check, but he didn't care. He was in no mood to get along.

"Anyway, we'll be out of your hair tomorrow."

"You're not in my hair," Michael replied through gritted teeth. "And you're welcome to stay all winter if you want."

"I'm not such a freeloader that I'd take advantage of your hospitality any longer than necessary. So just get off your high horse."

Taking up his hammer and saw, Michael stared at Andy for a moment. "I can see you're spoiling for a fight, and I'm not about to go along with that."

Andy gave a short laugh. "Probably just as well if you know what's good for you."

Emitting a frustrated growl, Michael dropped the tools. "What's bothering you, Andy? I thought you'd be happy now that the house is ready and the furniture is finished. You wanted to surprise Hope. And just when you're about to, you're acting like someone did you wrong."

"Nothing's wrong. Nothing you or anyone can fix, that is." He swiped at the sweat on his brow. And dropped onto the porch.

Michael joined him on the step. "I'd like to try and help."

"What could someone like you do?"

"Someone like me?" He gave a wary lift of his brow.

Andy drew a breath and as he expelled it, he knew he wasn't going to hold back. "You have everything a man could want. A beautiful wife and daughter, a son, and another child about to arrive any day. Ma worships the ground you walk on. You've made the farm a rousing success, even better than Pa ever did." He gave a mocking laugh. "What could you do to help me? You can't even understand me. Everything you touch turns to gold. Everything I touch is ruined." .

Silence hung between them for a moment. Then Michael's chest rose and fell with a heavy breath. "I do have a wonderful family. And I thank God for them. And Ma's happy in our home. She was a big help to me after Sarah died and Aimee was a baby. But she gives me what-for on a regular basis. And as for me having everything a man could want, it seems to me you do, too."

Andy started to rebut the statement, but stopped himself short of doing just that. How could he tell Michael that his marriage was a sham, that his stepchildren weren't his to raise, that his so-called wife slept as far away from him as she possibly could, although they'd finally agreed to share the bed—for sleeping only.

"You don't think you have a good life, Andy? Are you so ungrateful that you can't thank God for blessing you with a wonderful family?"

Disgust laced Michael's voice. But Andy was used to that. Used to disappointing his brother. Everyone, in fact. His entire life had been a disappointment. Until Yellow Bird came into it, then everything changed. Her love had made him a success. She loved him for the man he was and never once did he see that disappointment in her eyes. "You don't know everything, Michael."

"I guess not. But I know a man in love when I see one. I can also see that something's not right between you and Hope. But I don't suppose that's anyone's business but yours."

Andy stared. A man in love? He gave an inward laugh. A gleeful laugh at how wrong Michael was. Hope was a good woman, but he wasn't in love with her by any means. A frown puckered his brow as he thought for a second. "What do you mean you know a man in love? What am I doing?"

Michael chuckled. "You don't know?"

Andy glared. "Would I have asked?"

"A man doesn't work to build a home with such detail unless he loves the woman he's building it for. He doesn't work night and day to build nice furniture as a surprise."

"Any man would."

"You wouldn't."

Andy's ears warmed at the candid response. He couldn't blame his brother, really. The man Michael knew five years ago had never known the love of a woman. Had never held his dead baby in his hands. Hadn't lain in the gutter waiting to die. The Andy he'd known didn't exist anymore.

"I suppose you're right."

Michael grinned. "That was a little too easy."

Andy shrugged. He wouldn't deny loving Hope. Why intentionally shame a good woman? They'd all figure it out soon enough. After the spring thaw when he left. He'd decided to join up with another wagon train and offer his services as scout.

He was just about ready to suggest heading back to Michael's cabin when the sound of horse's hooves thundered toward them.

"It's Greg," Andy said, more to himself than Michael. "Something's wrong."

The boy reached them before they could speculate. He reined in the bay mare and took two gulping breaths.

"Take it easy, son," Andy said, grabbing the bridle. "What's wrong?"

"Miss Star."

Michael stepped forward. "Is she. . . ?"

Greg nodded and Michael ran to his horse. He untethered the black gelding and rode off at breakneck speed.

"Miss Star's having her baby, huh?"

"Yes, sir."

"You want to see the cabin?"

"Shouldn't we get back?"

Andy chuckled. "I don't think they need us there. As a matter of fact, I can almost guarantee you that they'll run us out of there as soon as we get there."

Gregory gave a sheepish grin.

Andy clapped him on the shoulder. "Come on. I'll show you, but you have to keep quiet about it. It's a surprise for your ma."

"Sure, Pa. . ."

Andy stopped dead in his tracks. He turned and stared at Greg.

The boy's face glowed red. "I'm sorry. It just came out, naturally. I didn't mean to."

Swallowing past a sudden lump in his throat, Andy fought the pleasure he'd received at hearing the unfamiliar title. He liked it. Too much.

Leveling a gaze at the boy, he could see the dread in Greg's face. Still, it had to be said. "You know how things are between your mother and me."

"Yeah," the boy muttered. "I just thought maybe things were different since we got to Oregon."

Instinctively, Andy knew he meant since he was sharing a room with Hope, but he didn't pursue the topic. Some things weren't suitable for a boy Greg's age.

"I think highly of her. And a finer woman I've never met."

"She's pretty, too." Greg glared at him, daring him to deny it. Andy almost chuckled to see a hint of the old Greg. He supposed he could bring out the worst in anyone.

"This isn't about how pretty she is. This is about our arrangement."

"You haven't told your family the truth."

"They'll know soon enough."

"When you leave, you mean?"

"Yes."

"Will your ma want us to stop calling her Grammy?"

"My leaving won't change anything for you, Greg. I married your ma legally. Nothing is going to change that either. Grammy is still your Grammy. Michael and Hank are still going to be your uncles."

"But you won't be our pa." The bitter edge in the boy's tone cut into Andy's conscience.

"Believe me, having those two as uncles is a lot better than having me as a pa."

"No one's a better pa than you."

The blade twisted inside Andy. He reached out and ruffled Greg's hair, which he now had to cut to keep shoulder length like Andy's. "If things were different, I'd be proud for a son like you."

"What things have to be different? Why can't you just stay? I know ma wishes you would."

Andy eyed the boy sharply. "Did she tell you that?"

"No. But I can tell she's taken a shine to you." His face grew red and Andy elbowed him.

"Ah, what do you know about women?"

Greg shrugged. "I know my ma."

"Maybe you do. But in this instance I think you're seeing what you want to see rather than what's actually there. Now, come on and let me show you the cabin."

Greg's nod was anything but enthusiastic.

Between Greg and Michael and God, Andy knew he was in for a long winter.

❧

Hope paced in front of the fire and tried to keep Michael

calm. Two days and still no baby.

Andy had finally admitted that the cabin was ready and had taken all the children there to wait out the labor. But before he left, he'd wandered about the cabin white-faced, and Hope knew he was reliving Yellow Bird's death delivering their baby.

Miss Hannah sat with Star. Hope stayed in the front room, trying to keep Michael occupied.

Michael dropped his head into his hands. "Why didn't I insist on finding a doctor by now?"

Hope went to him and knelt on the floor by his chair. Should she put her hand on his arm? The thought of touching a man who didn't belong to her in such an intimate manner made her stomach churn. When he started to cry, she pushed aside her modesty and placed an arm about his shoulders. "Shh. Michael, it'll be all right."

"She needs a doctor."

"Sometimes babies take awhile. Having a doctor here probably wouldn't make a difference at this point."

The door opened, bringing a gust of wind. Hope's pulse sped up at the sight of Andy. "I came to do chores," he said.

"Thanks." Michael's voice was muffled by his hands.

Andy beckoned her with the swoop of his hand. Hope accompanied him to the porch. "How is she?"

Tears sprang to Hope's eyes. "Getting weak. It's been too long."

"It's just like Yellow Bird."

"No, it isn't."

Tears shimmered in his eyes as he looked at her. "It feels like I'm living it all over again."

"Well, you're not, Andy." Hope's voice was sharper than she'd intended, but frustration and weariness dulled her sensitivity and bluntness took charge of her tongue. "This isn't about your wife and baby. This is about your brother and the fact that his wife may very well die if the baby doesn't come soon."

Tears slipped down Andy's cheek and soaked into his three-day-old beard.

Compassion replaced irritation, and Hope took him into her arms. He pressed his face into the curve of her neck and sobbed. Hope stroked his hair, running her fingers through the tresses.

"Shh, Andy. We have to pray. Remember when Greg took cholera? God did a miracle. We just have to pray for a miracle. That's all."

Grabbing her tighter, as though afraid she might try to pull away, Andy spoke into her ear. "But will He listen to someone like me?"

"You said only God could have led you to where the Indians had me that day. He heard your prayer then. Let's both pray."

Andy nodded against her shoulder. "God, please make the baby come." He barely uttered the words when sobs overtook him once more.

Tingles traveled up Hope's spine like butterfly wings against her skin.

"God," she whispered, suddenly shy. "The twins asked for miracles, and You gave several during the trail. And then when Greg was sick, You made him well when all the others died." Andy shuddered against her, and Hope caressed his hair like a child's. "We need to ask You to do a miracle for Star this time. Her baby is taking a long time to get here and I'm afraid her strength is almost gone. Andy and I are just asking for You to please do us another miracle. Make the baby come. Michael's a good man, but he needs his wife, and those two children of theirs need their mother. So we hope You'd like to do another miracle."

She pulled back and looked at Andy's tearstained face. "Do you feel better?"

He scowled.

"What?"

"You forgot to say amen."

Before she could reply, the door flew open and Michael stood wild-eyed. "Hope, Ma says come quick. The baby's coming."

fifteen

Hope's first sight of her new home stole her breath away. The log home stood beneath a harvest moon, the porch railings on her little cabin as regal to her as the most beautiful pillars on the most elegant mansion in Chicago—or anywhere for that matter.

"Oh, Andy. I love it."

He set the wagon brake and hopped down. Her heart skipped a beat when he held up his arms for her. Willingly, she slid into his embrace, her gaze never leaving his.

"Thank you," she whispered.

He kept her close and returned her stare. "I need to thank you for tonight."

"I didn't do anything, Andy."

"Yes, you did. You pulled me out of my past. When we started praying for Star, I finally let Yellow Bird and our baby go. I know I'll always have a place in my heart for them, but the grieving days are over."

Tears welled up in Hope's eyes. "Are you sure?"

"Yes." He held her tighter and dipped his head. "If you'll have me, I'd like to stay on here. To be a real husband to you and a pa to Gregory and Billy and Betsy."

Laughter bubbled to Hope's lips at the reality of the words she'd only dreamed of for months. "Oh, Andy. Are you sure?"

In answer, he swooped her into his arms and carried her up the steps and inside the cabin. "Your new home, Mrs. Riley."

Still reeling from being carried over the threshold like a new bride, Hope stared at the beautiful room. Her eyes widened. "I can't believe it!"

She'd expected to come home to bare rooms, needing to be filled. A fire in a lovely stone fireplace provided sufficient light to reveal a beautiful hand-carved rocking chair. "Put me down, Andy," she said, barely able to force the words through her tight throat.

When he complied, she walked across to the rocking chair and stroked the arms, the back, marveling at the softness of the wood.

"Wh–where did this come from?" She looked at Andy, then made a sweep of the room with her hand. "All of this?"

"I—" He cleared his throat.

Hope's jaw dropped as she realized the source of his embarrassment. "Are you saying you made these things?"

"I guess so."

She hurried to him and threw her arms around his neck. "Andy," she said over his shoulder. "This is wonderful. You have such talent. I had no idea you could do something like this."

He shrugged. "Just a hobby."

"A hobby?" She pulled away and held him at arm's length. "Do you realize how much people would pay in the city for handcrafted furniture? The quality is magnificent."

"I never really thought about it." He grinned. "You really think I could make a living at it?"

"Are you serious? Andy, look at this beautiful home. I'll be the envy of every woman for a hundred miles." She walked across to the table, in awe of the craftsmanship. Then her eyes found the corner and she gasped. A beautiful armoire occupied the space. "Oh, Andy." She walked toward the cabinet and opened the doors, revealing shelves and drawers. Though she'd had enough money to buy whatever kind of furniture she'd wanted to fill her home, nothing had ever compared to the magnificence of Oregon maple crafted into pieces of beauty.

"It has to be a Divine gift."

Andy fairly beamed under her praise, and Hope realized just how fragile her husband truly was. For some reason he didn't believe he had much worth.

She made a decision that she would work for the rest of her life to let him know what a treasure she considered him to be.

"Do you want to see the rest of the house?"

The low tone of his voice sent her heart racing, and she forgot about the rocking chair and the table and even the armoire. "Where are the children?"

"Asleep, I imagine. Hank's in the loft with the boys. Want to check on the girls?"

Keeping her gaze locked on his, she slowly shook her head.

"Are you sure?" She knew he wasn't asking about the children.

"I'm sure," she whispered, her love for him eclipsing her embarrassment at being so bold.

He closed the distance between them swiftly and took her in his arms. His lips closed over hers. She clung to him and returned his kiss with equal ardor. For the second time tonight, he swept her into his arms and carried her across a threshold.

⁂

"Where's Ma?"

Andy looked up from his coffee at the sound of Betsy's voice. "She's still sleeping. It was late when we got home from Uncle Michael's house."

Betsy grinned broadly, showing a missing eyetooth. "Did Aunt Star's baby come?"

"Sure did." He tweaked her nose. "A pretty little girl, but not quite as pretty as you."

Clapping happily, Betsy slid onto the bench. "We knew it would be a girl. Aimee wanted a baby sister so bad."

Andy chuckled and got up to pour himself another cup of coffee. One by one, the household began to stir. Aimee and her three-year-old little brother emerged from Betsy's bedroom. She squealed when Betsy told her the news about her baby sister.

Hank climbed down the loft ladder right ahead of Billy and Gregory.

When Hope finally appeared, Andy was tongue-tied. "Good morning, everyone." She smiled at the children, but didn't meet his eye. Tenderness turned in Andy's heart at her modesty. He'd never had much use for such things in women, but he found that he loved and admired it about Hope.

"Would you like a cup of coffee?" Andy asked.

"Thank you." She ducked her head, refusing to look at him while he poured.

"Would you like me to help with breakfast, Aunt Hope?" Aimee asked.

Silence hung like a blade over a chopping block. The twins exchanged glances, and Andy could see the ax was about to fall. If he didn't step in quick, Hope would be humiliated.

Andy cleared his throat. "Well, let me see. Since this is our first official family breakfast in our new home, I vote we let your Aunt Hope off the hook and I'll cook this morning.

"N—no, Andy. I'll cook."

"I don't mind."

She stood. "I can manage. Everyone go get dressed and make your beds, and I'll whip us up something in no time." She turned to Andy. "I guess I should ask if you were as competent at filling our food stores as you were about filling our home with furniture."

Andy felt his chest swell under her admiration and he was

relieved Michael had suggested just that thing.

"I still need to fill the smokehouse with meat, but that'll come after freeze up. I thought we'd buy a couple of hogs to slaughter. Until then, I can shoot whatever we need daily. I have some bacon that Michael gave us to see us through until we can replenish. Ma gave us a couple of her laying hens. I've already gathered eggs." He motioned to a bowl of eggs on the counter. "And Ma sent over a couple of loaves of bread."

She swallowed hard. "Sounds good. I'm sure you have chores to do, so don't let me be keeping you."

"I'll just bring in that bacon first."

She gave him a distracted nod, and Andy knew she was concentrating on her upcoming task.

Hank rose, draining his cup. He swallowed and grinned. "Nothing I like better than bacon and eggs for breakfast. I'll just help Andy with those chores. That'll work up a hearty appetite, so be sure and cook plenty." He gave her an affectionate brotherly peck on the cheek.

Andy chuckled. She seemed determined to fix breakfast herself, so maybe Ma had taught her a thing or two in the weeks they'd been at Michael's. He cast one last glance at her before he went outside. He hoped so, anyway.

An hour later, he stared at black bacon and runny eggs and realized that of all the wonderful qualities his wife possessed, cooking wasn't one of them.

Silence reigned supreme over the table, no one daring to make a peep. Andy ventured a glance at Hope. As though feeling his attention, she looked up, burst into tears, and ran for the bedroom.

Andy stood. He strode across the room and muscled Hope's rocking chair in his arms. Then he walked toward the door. "I have to go to town. You girls clean the dishes while I'm gone. I should be back before lunchtime."

Hank stood. "I'll saddle up and ride with you. What are you doing with the chair?"

"My business."

"Fair enough."

Once they got outside, Hank turned to him. "Hope going to be okay?"

"She'll be all right."

"I don't think I've ever met a woman who couldn't cook."

Andy frowned. "Well, now you have. Nothing wrong with that. I'm not much of a farmer like most men."

"You'll have to learn to be a farmer now, won't you?" Hank chuckled. "Unless you want to take up another line of work, say preaching."

"I'm willing to become the best farmer in Oregon for Hope's sake."

"Whew, you really have changed."

"Just wait, little brother. When you meet up with the right woman, you'd be willing to give up just about anything to make her happy."

Hank's face reddened.

Andy laughed. "Who is she, Reverend?"

"What do you mean?" he asked a little too innocently.

"My guess is you've already taken a shine to some lady."

"All right. I have. But I don't think she feels the same way."

"Have you asked her?"

"Of course not. I would never put her in the position of having to reject me. That might hamper our friendship. And I don't want to risk it."

"The woman in question wouldn't happen to be a certain seamstress would it?"

Though Andy didn't think it was possible, Hank's face grew redder making his freckles pop out. But he didn't deny it. "Rosemary."

"Don't wait too long to talk to her, Hank. Time is too precious to waste."

Inwardly, Andy chuckled that he was giving anyone advice on love. He supposed once a man finally stopped struggling against it and found the woman who was meant just for him, he just wanted everyone to be as happy as he was.

He hooked up the team while Hank saddled his horse.

Though he hated to drive the wagon, the task he had in mind required that he do so. Despite his preference for riding on horseback, he had to remember he was doing this for Hope, the woman he loved. A wide grin spread across his lips as he imagined the look on her face when she saw her surprise.

❧

When Hope finally got up the gumption to leave her bedroom, she was happy to find the kitchen clean and the children playing quietly in the living room. Gregory had even kept a fire going to ward off the autumn chill.

"Where's your pa?" she asked.

Gregory sent her a sharp glance. "Town."

"Did he say when he was coming home?"

"Before lunch."

"Aunt Hope. When may I go home and see my little sister?" Aimee asked.

"I don't know, sweetheart. I suppose your pa will come after you sometime today."

"What did mama name her?"

So much had happened since Hope had given the baby girl her first bath, she had to stop and think hard for a moment. Then it came back to her. "Oh yes. Hannah." She laughed. "How could I forget that? They named her after your Grammy."

The girls giggled. "Grammy has such a pretty name, don't you think, Betsy?"

"My favorite name ever!"

"Hannah Riley." Aimee dimpled. "My favorite name, too."

Hope filled the coffeepot with water from the bucket on the counter. Andy would be home soon and she at least wanted to present him with hot coffee to warm him after a chilly ride to town and back.

Listening to the girls chatter about the new baby, Hope smiled to herself. Perhaps this time next year, she'd be holding a new baby of her own. She felt a sudden shiver of glee at the thought of giving Andy his own child. She found herself praying another prayer. *Please, let me give him a baby.*

sixteen

"I can't tell you how happy I am to see you, Mr. Riley. That Mrs. Barker is a regular sea captain. Hollering about this and that. I don't know how she stays in business."

Andy grinned at Lucille's attempt to keep her voice down, but from the doorway, he heard Mrs. Barker's loud harrumph.

Lucille shrugged. "How is Mrs. Riley?"

"Fine. But she's ready for you to come to the house. We only have half the loft for you to sleep in for now. But we'll build you a room of your own come spring."

"Believe me, half a loft will seem like a palace compared to living in this prison."

Lucille's exaggeration elicited a chuckle from Andy.

"How long until you can be ready to go?"

"I best give the room a good going over before I leave. I'd hate for that woman to besmirch my name after I'm gone and tell people I didn't keep a tidy room."

"An hour?"

"That'll be fine."

"All right. I'll be back then."

Andy's next stop was the general store. The smell of leather oil and pipe tobacco greeted him when he stepped through the door. Andy walked up to the counter where a black-haired customer leaned easily against the counter, dressed in a black suit of clothes that spoke of privilege.

The proprietor placed his hands flat on the counter. "What can I do for you?"

"I. . .um. . ." Andy cleared his throat. His palms were damp and his heart beat a rapid rhythm within his chest. Trying to procure honest work was going to be harder than he'd thought it would be.

"Well?"

The owner's prodding brought Andy back to his senses.

"I make furniture."

"I have a good supply of nails over on that table."

"No. I didn't want to buy nails. Well, actually, I could probably use some. Just finished building my wife's cabin."

"Congratulations," he replied, without much enthusiasm. "As I mentioned, nails are over there."

Stalling, Andy grabbed two bags of nails. He paid for them and stuffed them inside his coat pocket. The little man behind the counter gave him a questioning look. "Well? Anything else I can do for you?"

Embarrassment crept up Andy's neck. "To be honest, I'd like to sell some of the furniture I build, and I thought you might be interested in placing it in your store for a percentage. I have a sample in the wagon just outside, if you'd like to take a look."

The other man at the counter followed Andy's pointing finger. Andy scowled at him. Obviously taking the hint, the man gave a curt nod and headed for the door.

Turning back to the proprietor, Andy waited while he seemed to be considering the proposition. Andy held his breath.

The little man finally nodded. "Can't hurt to take a look. I'm not making any promises, though."

"I understand."

Andy's heart thundered in his ears while the man examined Hope's rocking chair.

"This is better than average work." The man stroked his chin. "How much you asking for it?"

"This one belongs to my wife, so it isn't for sale, but I can make another one, and if you'll display it, I'll give you a percentage."

"I might be interested. What else do you make?"

Andy went down a list.

"Well, come inside, and I'll write up an agreement for us both to sign."

Excitement nearly exploded in Andy's chest as he followed the man inside. Hope had been right. Perhaps he could make a living doing what he loved to do.

After the man wrote up a rough contract of sorts, he pushed it across the counter. They haggled a moment about percentage until they came to a satisfactory compromise. Andy signed and pushed the paper back.

The proprietor started to sign then looked up, his expression suddenly hard, his eyes firing anger. "You Andy Riley?"

"That's right."

"The name Johnny Harper ring a bell?"

"I haven't heard it in quite a few years, but yeah, I used to know Johnny." Andy had met Johnny the first year in Oregon. He'd just been about Gregory's age at the time. The young man had taught Andy how to smoke and drink whiskey.

Johnny had tried to talk Andy into robbing the bank with him, but Andy's conscience wouldn't allow such a bold act. Johnny had gotten caught. He tried to pin it on Andy, but thankfully, Andy been home with his parents at the time, attending a picnic with neighbors.

"How do you know Johnny?" Andy finally replied.

"You don't recognize me, eh? He was my boy." The man's eyes grew misty.

"Was?"

"He was sent to prison for the robbery. After he got out, he was more of an outlaw than when he went in. He was finally hanged."

"I'm so sorry, Mr. Harper. I didn't know."

"How could you have known?" The man's bitter tone caused Andy's heart to sink. He didn't even recognize the man, he'd grown so old in the last eighteen years. But clearly, he still believed Johnny's original claim—that Andy was the real thief.

"I am sorry about Johnny, Mr. Harper. I didn't know him for very long."

"Just long enough to turn him down the wrong path." The man's bitter response cut into Andy's sense of hope. "Get out of my store before I put a bullet in you."

Andy walked in bewildered silence into the cold November air. He shivered as a blast of wind slipped under his collar. But the chilly air didn't even come close to the icy chill invading his heart.

He climbed into the wagon. Hope had been wrong. He'd tried to do right by her. Had wanted to come home with the news that he would be building and selling furniture, as she'd been so sure he should. But how could she have known that a man couldn't escape who he was.

Loud music and shrill laughter reached his ears from the saloon down the street. Andy's mouth suddenly went dry. His heart rate increased. He hadn't been tempted to drink in months. But now he could almost feel the burning sensation of whisky in his throat. Could almost sense the welcome, numbing fog that would soon follow. Abruptly, he maneuvered the horses in front of the saloon. He didn't allow second thoughts. This was the only life he'd ever know. What was the point in trying to be anything more?

He hesitated only a second as Hope's face shot through his mind. The sweetness with which she'd given herself to him the night before. Rather than dissuade him, the image spurred him forward in frustration. He would never be good enough for a woman like Hope. Should never have thought to try to be a family man like Michael.

He reached for the door.

"Andy?"

A growl escaped Andy's throat at being detained from his mission. He turned to face Hank.

Hank narrowed his gaze, his eyes stormy. "What are you doing?"

"You're a smart man, figure it out."

Hank quickly closed the distance between them and stood between Andy and the saloon entrance.

"Get out of my way, Hank."

"I can't let you do it."

"You don't have any choice."

Hank folded his arms across his chest. He stood several inches shorter than Andy and was more wiry than muscular. Andy knew he could take him if he needed to, but he wouldn't. How could he blame Hank for looking out for his best interests? He knew his brother would stay planted in front of that door until he knocked him out of the way or gave in. How badly did he really want to go into that saloon? He studied the determination in his brother's face, the sincerity in his eyes, and Andy's fight left him.

He clapped Hank on the shoulder. "You win, little brother."

Relief washed Hank's face. "Do you want to talk about it?"

"Naw, I'll be all right. Listen, Hank, I need a favor."

"What's that?"

"Take the wagon and go get Lucille from the boardinghouse."

"The woman Hope brought west with her?"

Andy nodded. "She's ready to come to the cabin, and I told her I'd pick her up in an hour. I have some things to do, first."

Suspicion clouded Hank's eyes. "Like what?"

"Don't worry. I'm not going into the saloon."

With a look that clearly said he wasn't so sure Andy was telling the truth, Hank gave a hesitant nod. "All right. Use my horse."

Hank climbed into the wagon.

Andy extended his arm. "Thanks, Hank."

Nodding, Hank clasped the hand. He held on. "Are you sure you're okay, Andy? Do you want to go over to the church and talk about it?"

"No. I need time alone." He hesitated a minute, then decided to come clean. "I'm going up to Pike's cabin. Do you still want me to take the horse?"

"Go ahead. I'll get one from Michael. But you shouldn't go up there now. Before long the pass will be too dangerous for you to go through until after the spring thaw."

Andy nodded. "That's what I'm counting on. Do you need your saddlebag?"

Hank scowled and shook his head impatiently. "There's only one thing in there and you need it more than I do. What about Hope and the children?"

"They have enough wood cut to last the winter, enough food except for meat and Gregory's pretty near as good a shot as I am. They won't go hungry."

"Maybe it's not so much about hunger as needing a man in the house. You know how winters can be. Do you really want your wife and children to be alone?"

Like an arrow, his words struck their mark, but Andy's mind was already made up. He would never be the man Hope believed he could be. Today's fiasco had proven that. "Will you give Hope a message for me?"

"If you're determined to do this thing, then I suppose I have no choice."

"Tell her I meant everything from the bottom of my heart. And I'm sorry."

"Andy, don't do something you'll regret."

"Good-bye."

Andy watched the wagon until it rolled out of sight, then, without another glance at the saloon, he mounted Hank's horse and rode out of town, in the opposite direction that his heart wanted to go.

❧

For three days straight, Hope lay in bed, nursing her grief. She felt like a fool for believing a word he'd said. Her face burned at the memory of their night together. How eager she'd been. Wherever he was, he must be laughing at her for being an idiot. And she couldn't blame him.

A knock at the door interrupted her self-deprecating thoughts. Irritation bit her. In no mood to be bothered, she ignored the knock.

A moment later, the door swung open. "What do you think you're doing in bed?"

Hope sat up, smoothing her hair, although after three days without a brush there wasn't much point. "Miss Hannah!"

Miss Hannah looked down at her and the outrage on her plump face turned to pity. "Oh, honey." The mattress sank beneath her weight as she sat. She took Hope into her comforting arms. Without a word, Hope let loose a flood of tears. Great, wrenching sobs shook her. When finally her tears were spent, she snatched her hanky from the bedside table.

"I can't believe he left."

"Wasn't that the plan all along?"

A gasp escaped her lips. "You knew?"

Miss Hannah nodded. "Greg spilled it."

"I'm seriously regretting ever teaching that child to speak!"

A chuckle left Miss Hannah's throat. "That's good. You still have a sense of humor."

"Anyway, Andy wasn't supposed to leave until spring at least.

And after the other night, I thought. . .I mean, he said—"

Hope twisted the hanky between her fingers, facing flushing hot at what she'd almost revealed.

"I see. . ."

"Oh, Miss Hannah. I miss him. I never thought I'd fall in love. But it hit me so fast. Almost from the moment I met Andy. Even when he was stinking and barely recognizable from the beating he took."

Miss Hannah's face blanched. "Maybe you should tell me everything from the beginning."

Slowly, Hope started from the time she found Andy in the alley. She told about Gregory's trouble, and the miracles that occurred. The older woman's eyes misted, and she grabbed her own hanky from her wristband when Hope told her about Yellow Bird and the little grandbaby Miss Hannah would never hold in her comforting arms. And finally, she told of Andy asking her to take him as a real husband.

"Oh, I'm so stupid for believing him!" She smacked the bed in frustration.

"Andy's been running for a long, long time. I've plumb wore out my knees praying for him."

"Do you think if I pray for another miracle, God might send him home?"

"Maybe, but Hope, you know God isn't just up there doling out miracles to suit us. As much as He wants to bless us, the most important thing is the miracle of new life."

"You mean, you think I could be carrying Andy's child?"

Miss Hannah chuckled. "Well, you'd know more about that than I would. I'm not talking about human life. I'm talking about a new spiritual life."

"Like asking Jesus into your heart?"

"Exactly like that."

"I've been studying the Bible, Miss Hannah. For over a

month, I've been listening to Hank at church and reading the Bible. I'm just not sure it's all true. D—do you think that's why God sent Andy away? Because I didn't pray the prayer with Betsy?"

"No, I don't. But the very fact that you asked me the question proves that you do believe and are just resisting."

Hope couldn't deny that her heart stirred every time she read the Bible.

"So if I surrender and ask Jesus in my heart, do you think God will do another miracle for me and send Andy home?"

"What would you do if He didn't? Would you still believe in Him, or would you decide there's nothing to Christianity after all?"

Hope considered the question. "I don't really know."

"You see, Jesus wants a relationship with you. How would you feel if your children only came to you when they needed something?"

Knowing Miss Hannah didn't expect an answer, Hope kept silent and pondered her words.

"God sent His Son to die so that humanity could be reconciled back to fellowship with Him."

"I thought it was so we didn't go to hell."

"That's the end result of knowing Jesus. Heaven. But most of us have a lot of living to do between now and then. God wants to be involved with our daily lives, our struggles, and our joys." She brought the hanky up for a quick swipe across her nose. "Yes, he wants to perform miracles for us. But sometimes we have to struggle. Those are the times when we really learn to trust God. To have faith that even if things don't turn out the way we expect or hope they will, we still have a God who loves us and who wants to hold us while the hurting lasts."

"So you're saying that Andy might not come back, even if I pray?"

"Honey, I've been praying for my son all of his life. He's been gone for the better part of fifteen years."

Dread clenched Hope's heart at the thought of Andy leaving and staying gone forever.

As if sensing her need to be alone, Miss Hannah rose quietly. "I'll be here when you're ready to come out and face the world."

"Thank you, Miss Hannah. Please tell Lucille you'll be staying to supper."

"Who do you think sent for me?"

Hope smiled. "Lucille's a real gem."

"So are you, Hope. And I hope Andy figures that out and comes back."

Tears filled Hope's eyes once more, and her throat clogged as Miss Hannah shut the door behind her.

Left alone, Hope felt the solitude through and through. Was Jesus really able to fill that emptiness for her? Would He even want to? Somehow, she found herself on her knees beside the bed. She closed her eyes and said the only thing that came to mind. "Jesus."

Suddenly, a sob began deep within and shot from her lips almost of its own volition. But once the sobbing began, it continued. Deep and painful wails that cried of her shame, her sins, her deep desire to know Jesus the way Miss Hannah knew Him, and Gregory and Betsy, and even Billy.

As the weeping gave way to gentle tears of surrender, Hope understood Betsy's joy. She understood why Miss Hannah could still believe in Jesus when her prayers for her son seemed to go unanswered year after year. She understood that Jesus loved Andy even more than she did, and that He, too, wept over His lost love.

seventeen

Andy rode for a full day to reach the cabin. Snow made the ride slow going as the horse slipped and slid up the mountain. Andy knew that, in another week or two, Hank's prediction would come true and the pass would be too dangerous to ride through.

With mounds of snow flanking the narrow trail that allowed for passage through the mountains, one slip of a horse's hooves or a sneeze could start an avalanche. More than one man had been buried alive for his folly.

On Andy's first day of solitude, he used the ax found inside the cabin and chopped enough wood to last several weeks. The cabin had once been used by trappers, but now stood pretty much for anyone who needed a place to hole up.

The second day, he brought down a deer with one shot. Days three, four, and five, he stared at the fire and thought about his wife and children. A lonely ache began in the pit of his stomach and combined with his boredom to create a healthy dose of frustration.

On day six, a very real feeling that he was going mad led him to Hank's Bible. He was willing to do anything to occupy his mind. He flipped through the pages until he found something familiar. He read about Noah and the ark. Next, he started reading about David and read all the way from the shepherd boy's time in the fields tending his flock to the king's death. Andy read and read and reread for two weeks, avoiding the four gospels at all costs.

After a month, his beard had grown out fully.

Three days of blizzard-like conditions had kept him inside and he felt restless. Grabbing his rifle, he followed deer tracks in the snow until he spied a massive buck standing in the distance. He took a step forward and heard a *snnnnaaaap*. Pain cut into his leg like no pain he'd ever experienced.

Sinking to the ground, he screamed out as the snow stained crimson.

Andy had always heard when a man faced sudden death, he repented for all of his wickedness. For Andy, this proved to be true. Blood flowed quickly, and the pain soon became more than he could bear. Waves of dizziness overcame him. He surrendered to unconsciousness breathing one name, "Jesus."

❧

Andy woke to the soft hum of voices. For the second time in less than a year, he'd passed out expecting that he'd never wake up. He could smell the wood smoke and knew he had been rescued.

This is the second time You've spared my life, God. Is it even possible that You have a purpose for me?

He craned his neck to locate his rescuer but was unable to see who had saved him. Pain shot through his leg as he rolled to get a better view. He groaned.

"Do not move." The soft voice was urgent.

A trace of shock slithered through him. "Yellow Bird?" Perhaps he had gone to heaven, after all.

She stood over him, her silky black hair brushing his arm. "You must lie still or your leg will reopen."

Tears filled Andy's eyes. "You're not Yellow Bird."

The young Indian woman gave him a sympathetic smile. "No, I am not. I am Little Moon."

A bearded buckskin-clad man came to stand behind the young woman, towering above her like a grizzly standing next to an average-sized man. The man's gentle voice belied his massive size. "Someone was looking out for you, little brother."

"What happened?"

"I'm ashamed to say the snow covered my trap."

"And my leg found it?"

"Yes. My wife and I found you just in time. It's been a fight with all the blood you lost."

"How long have I been here?"

The young woman held up three fingers. "Now I will bring you soup to make you strong."

The thought of food curled Andy's stomach, but the Indian woman waved away his protest. "You must eat."

The determination in her tone left no room for argument. "Yes, ma'am."

"You called my wife Yellow Bird."

"I'm sorry. For a second, she. . .uh. . .reminded me of someone I once knew."

"And loved?"

"Yes. For a very short time."

"My name's Hal Fulton. Little Moon has been my wife for a little over five years. Don't ask me what she sees in an old mountain man like me, but I thank God daily for sending her to me."

The young Indian woman returned with a bowl. She gave her husband an indulgent smile. "I see his beautiful heart. And I know this is the man God has made for me."

Taken aback by the easy way she spoke about God, Andy couldn't help but question her. "How do you know about the white man's God?"

She narrowed her gaze and straightened her shoulders. "God so loved *all* of the world that He gave His Son. He does not belong to white men only."

Andy felt his neck warm. "I didn't mean to insult you. I know God wants to be a God to all mankind. But my experience with Indians has taught me that most tribes serve their own gods and don't believe in Jesus."

She nodded soberly. "This is true. But my mother was a white woman captured by my father. She taught my father the ways of the true God." She smiled, her eyes alight with joy. "He became a Christian and offered to take her home to her people, but she loved him and chose to live in the village."

Andy couldn't help but respond to her warmth.

"Now, no more talking. You must eat and then rest. And eat again, and rest again. And soon you will be strong."

❧

Andy had been gone two months when Hope knew for sure. She was carrying his child. Excitement and dread combined with her already heightened emotions and she often found herself reduced to tears. They spent Christmas with Andy's family at Michael's home.

Miss Hannah's eyes misted when Hope revealed her condition, but made her promise not to tell anyone else for now, until she'd had a chance to share it with the children. Miss Hannah had promised. But she squeezed Hope's hand and whispered, "Maybe now God will bring Andy home."

Hope smiled tenderly at her mother-in-law. "But even if He doesn't, God will take care of us."

That had been two months ago. Now, four months pregnant, headaches, nausea, fatigue, and constant snowstorms confined her inside. Depression set in, driving her to her bed most days, wondering what kind of fool she was to travel more than halfway across the country only to be left alone in this forsaken place. Today happened to be one of those days. She hadn't left her bed all day.

A knock at her door drew her from the monotony of staring at the log walls wondering what she'd ever seen in Andy Riley. "Yes?"

Gregory entered, carrying a tray. "I brought you some supper, Ma."

One look at her handsome son and she remembered exactly why she'd come here. And she'd do it all over again. A smile formed from deep inside her and found its way to her lips.

"Thank you, son. But I think I'll eat with the rest of you tonight. I have a wonderful announcement to make."

She brushed her hair, changed her clothes, and sat at the head of the table.

Glancing about at the expectant faces, she gathered a breath for courage and forged ahead. "I'm going to have a baby."

Unabashed joy lit Betsy's face. "You mean it?" She jumped up from her seat and flung her arms around Hope's neck.

Hope laughed. "Yes, I mean it."

"When?"

"August."

Billy gave her a shy grin. "Is it a boy or a girl?"

"We'll know in about five months, won't we?"

"I hope it's a boy."

Hope turned her attention to Gregory. "You're awfully quiet. What do you think?"

The look of utter betrayal on his face hit Hope with a force and her heart nearly broke.

His questioning gaze sought hers. "How could he just leave?"

"He didn't know, Greg."

"But h—he lied to me. He told me it was just a business arrangement."

Hope's cheeks blazed. "That's between Andy and me."

"Yes, Ma," he muttered and stared down at his plate.

"Will Andy come back now, Ma?" Billy asked.

"I don't know, son. But if not, we'll be okay."

"I miss him," Betsy broke in.

They hadn't spoken of him in so long, Hope had begun to wonder if they even really remembered him, though she knew that couldn't be the case.

"I miss him too, Bets. We just need to pray that wherever he is, God is taking care of him."

Greg hopped up. "I have to go do chores."

Her heart nearly breaking, Hope watched him go. *Father, please watch over Greg. And don't let Andy stay gone so long that he does irreparable damage to his relationship with Greg. If he comes back at all.*

How she wanted to get word to him somehow that he had a child coming. But even though Hank knew where he was, the pass would be closed for another two months at least, Hank assured her. So there would be no getting word to him, anyway. And he might be long gone before anyone could find him.

Besides, Hope wanted him to come home because his heart was sending him, not because of guilt or duty. If he didn't love her and want to be her husband, then she didn't want him to come back.

She'd lived through one loveless marriage. The only thing different had been that she didn't love her husband either, though she'd had respect for him as a man and for his position. But she was desperately, whole-heartedly in love with Andy. And she knew she couldn't settle for part of him. She'd have his heart. Or nothing.

eighteen

Andy mended slowly, but thanks to Little Moon applying poultices and dried herbs, infection was minimal and he recovered with full use of his leg. Rather than helping him back to his cabin, Hal and Little Moon insisted he wait out the winter with them.

Remembering the mind-numbing boredom of that first month in the mountains, he quickly agreed.

He moved to a thick bed of buffalo hides, and Little Moon hung a blanket to enclose the corner sleeping area she shared with her husband.

Once he was able to join Hal, they spent their days looking after Hal's traps, evenings reading Scripture or discussing something they'd read.

"The pass will be opening up in another month or two, little brother," Hal observed one evening over supper."

"Yeah, I guess so." Andy liked the way Hal always called him little brother. He quickly understood that Hal saw him as a brother in Christ. As their relationship had deepened into friendship, so had Andy's relationship with God.

He couldn't very well deny God anymore. Not after God had twice saved him from certain death. Andy spent many hours reading the Bible, taking questions to Hal, and learning to pray. He knew that he was a different man inside than the man who had been caught in that trap weeks ago.

"So, when the pass opens, will you be headed for home?"

Andy couldn't help but grin over his friend's attempt to gather information. So far, Andy hadn't felt like he could open up. It wasn't that he didn't want to. As a matter of fact, he'd come to appreciate Hal's wisdom on many subjects. Perhaps, that was the reason he didn't want to admit to all his past doings. And for leaving Hope and the children the way he had. Could he take the chance at reading disappointment in Hal's eyes?

He shrugged. "Maybe."

"Little Moon thinks you're still pining away for Yellow Bird."

"Yellow Bird?"

"You talked about her the first night."

He remembered. And for a few nights after that, her memory had invaded his mind, most likely because of Little Moon's ministrations. He hadn't spent any time with an Indian woman since leaving the Sioux village.

But soon the memory faded again, to be replaced by Hope's image. If he was pining for anyone, it was for his wife.

Hal's chuckle brought him back to the present. "I think Little Moon is right. She suggested we take you along with us when we go back to the Indian village. Perhaps one of the young women will take a liking to you, too. If a grizzly bear like me can be blessed enough to find a woman like my Little Moon, I'm sure a handsome fella like yourself can catch someone's eye."

Taken aback by the suggestion, Andy couldn't speak. When the silence became uncomfortable, Little Moon cleared her throat softly. "Perhaps Andy does not wish to find another Indian woman."

"Oh, it isn't that." He had no desire to insult the woman who had taken such good care of him and nursed him back to health. "It's just. . .well, to tell you the truth, Yellow Bird has been dead for several years. I have a new wife now. Her name is Hope."

Hal's laughter fairly shook the cabin. "Well, why didn't you just say so? You must be awful lonesome for her."

Andy nodded. "I am."

Little Moon frowned. She put her hand on her husband's arm. "Something is not right between you and your wife, Andy?"

How did women always know these things?

Andy shrugged.

Hal leaned forward. "Maybe you'd better tell us what the problem is. I've been told I'm a pretty good listener. And I can vouch for Little Moon, too."

Knowing the time had come to share his story didn't make it any easier. He pushed back his bowl and gathered a slow breath. "I'll start when Yellow Bird died. She was my wife and was carrying our only child. . . ."

Andy felt the irony that a story six years in the making only took moments to tell. He capped off the story by telling about the incident with Mr. Harper in the general store. And, finally, of his flight to the mountains to escape his inability to be a man Hope could be proud of.

Little Moon wiped her eyes. "You must return to Hope. She will love you for the man you are."

A glimmer of hope rose and fell almost simultaneously. "I've made so many mistakes."

"Well, she knew that when she decided to be your wife." Hal's gentle voice held a note of compassion.

"What does your heart tell you, Andy?"

"I know God has forgiven me of all my past mistakes. But what if I can't be the kind of man Hope deserves?"

Little Moon reached across the table and took his hand. "This woman loves you. She knew the man you are when she shared your bed. You've broken her heart by leaving her. That is what you will have to work to mend before anything else.

Trust God to make you worthy of her."

"My wife is a smart woman, little brother. If you have any sense, you'll listen to her." Hal beamed with love for Little Moon. She sent him a tender smile.

Watching the interaction of this couple who loved each other so madly, he suddenly knew he would go home and make things right. No matter how long it took or what he had to do or where he had to sleep, he was determined to win Hope's love once more.

One thing he knew. The next few weeks until the pass opened were going to be the longest of his life.

&

Hope took not-so-secret joy in tending her very first garden. Michael had plowed a spot off to the side of her house, and Star had come to teach her to plant. She couldn't believe how many details there were to attend to. Learning the difference between weeds and shoots. It was enough to keep her mind occupied.

Now she sat on the ground, pulling weeds—at least she hoped they were weeds.

"Company's coming, Ma," Greg called from where he stood over the pig trough dumping food for the hogs.

She followed the direction of Greg's gaze and her heart nearly stopped. Even at a distance, she'd recognize that posture. "Andy," she whispered.

Apparently, the idea occurred to Greg, as well, for he took off at a run toward Andy. Hope had no idea what to expect. Her heart sank when the boy started yelling. "You can't come back! We don't need you."

Andy dismounted and clapped his hand on Greg's shoulder. "I know I did you wrong, son."

"I ain't your son. You didn't want me to call you Pa, remember?" He threw off Andy's hand and continued to glare.

Giving a solemn nod, Andy continued to regard the boy with patience. "I've spent all winter thinking about you. And about things I said and did. I came to ask your ma and you children to forgive me. If you'll take me back, I promise I'll never leave again."

Hope could see the struggle in Greg's face. She understood, for she felt the same struggle. The boy hesitated and she thought he might not forgive Andy. But in a split-second, he flung his arms about him.

"I'd be honored if you'd call me Pa," Andy said still holding the boy.

Hope stepped forward as Gregory stepped out of Andy's arms. Andy's eyes grew wide as his gaze took in her figure. She felt the blush rise to her face. "Greg, will you please go inside and keep the twins occupied while your pa and I have a talk?"

Apprehension covered Andy's features at her words. When Greg was in the house with the door shut, Hope regarded Andy frankly. "What made you decide to come back?"

"A lot of things." He motioned to her stomach. "Are we having a baby?"

"Yes. Why did you run away the day after?"

"Let's get you off your feet and I'll tell you everything, all right?" Warmth enveloped her arm as he took her elbow and led her to the porch.

She settled in, enjoying the experience of being taken care of.

For the next several minutes, Andy opened up about all the events that happened after he left the cabin that morning.

She gasped when he told of his accident. But she thanked God when he told of being rescued. When he got to his renewed relationship with the Lord, she wept.

"Your mother will be so blessed to know her prayers have finally been answered. And Andy, you needn't have left. A man came around the day after and asked for you. Apparently, he'd coerced Mr. Harper into giving him your name and pointing him to your ma, who pointed him up here. He said he saw your work and wanted to hire you to make the furniture for a new hotel he's building. He only wanted the best, but handmade furniture would be a good advertising tool for the hotel."

"Ah well, it's probably too late."

"That's the beauty of it, Andy. It's not. He was traveling back to Boston and said he'd be back this spring sometime when they actually start building the hotel. He hoped you'd be available to discuss terms when he returned."

A grin tipped Andy's lips. "And will I be?"

She looked out over their fields, freshly planted by hired help. "Just look at that beautiful land." She glanced at him and grinned. "And get used to looking at it, because you're going to be here for a very, very long time, Andy Riley."

His eyes filled with tears and he took her face in his hands. "I know I don't deserve this second chance. But I'll make sure you don't regret it."

Leaning in, he took her lips with his and for Hope it was as though she, herself, had come home again. Just as Andy deepened his kiss and moved closer to her, the baby kicked hard. He jumped back. "What was that?"

"What do you think?"

Awe covered his features. He started to reach toward her stomach, then drew his hand back and met her gaze. "May I?"

"Of course."

The baby rewarded him with several kicks. Overcome with emotion, Andy gathered Hope in an embrace that nearly took her breath away.

He leaned back and held her at arm's length. "It's like I've been given a second chance with my entire life. God, you, the baby, the furniture business. I'm almost worried it won't last."

Hope laughed and pressed her palm to his perpetually scratchy cheek. "Don't worry about anything, Andy. God has chosen to give you a second chance for a reason."

Andy covered her hand with his and gazed at her with such an intensity of emotion, he almost stole Hope's breath away. "I love you, Hope Riley. I missed you while I was gone, but I'm glad God sent me to the mountains so He could reach me." He turned her palm over and kissed it. "I could never have been a good husband, no matter how much I loved you, until I gave my life fully to God and left the past behind."

Tears sprang into Hope's eyes. "Oh, Andy."

He kissed her once more, and she yielded easily. She sent a hasty prayer of thanks heavenward. She looked to the future with anticipation and hope. When they broke the kiss, they were both breathless.

Andy smiled at her and kissed her nose. He turned to look across the field, and Hope saw the spark of pride in his eyes.

"Beautiful, aren't they?"

"They are. Fresh and green and full of promise."

"I don't pretend to know what God has planned for our lives, but one thing I do know. . .our best days are still to come."

Slipping his arm about her, Andy pulled Hope close to his side and looked down at her. "Our best days are still to come."

He brought his face close to hers once more. And when he kissed her, Hope knew that for them both, the past was gone and the only thing that mattered was the future God had set before them.

When Andy let her go, she sighed and snuggled into his embrace. As they watched the beautiful sunset, Hope thanked God for the joy of today and the hope for tomorrow.

epilogue

Weddings always made her cry. Hope sniffled, tears stinging her eyes as she watched Gregory smile tenderly at the bride. Her heart nearly burst with love and motherly pride. He'd come such a long way from the troubled boy he'd once been. Only God could have brought about such a magnificent change.

He had even finally cut his hair. Another sign of maturity as he didn't wish to offend anyone. Especially the members of his new little flock.

No one had thought it would ever happen, but after twenty years of secretly loving each other, Rosemary and Hank were finally tying the knot. And Gregory was performing his first act as pastor of the church in Hobbs—officiating the nuptials. Andy sniffled beside her. She gave her husband a tender smile and pressed her handkerchief into his hand.

"Sawdust from these new benches," he said gruffly, denying his tears.

Hope nodded and squeezed his hand. She understood her husband's emotion, his pride in the son he'd raised. Gregory stood so handsome and tall, a man of God, wholly committed to the calling he felt so strongly.

Fifteen-year-old Eva squirmed on Hope's other side. "When's it going to be over, Ma?"

Hope silenced the girl with a stern frown. Eva was her father's child through and through. She'd inherited his reddish-brown hair and brown eyes. Lashes that brushed her cheeks when she closed her eyes. And a dimple next to her lip that crinkled every time she laughed. Oh, the girl was a charmer.

Hope worried over her free spirit, though. She moved with the same recklessness that had once controlled Andy. Hope only prayed that God would get hold of the girl before she grew to be a woman. She prayed that Eva be spared the heartaches her pa had been forced to endure because of his unwillingness to allow God to temper his wild spirit.

For now, Hope kept her close. She had a few more years to try to temper her. Beyond that, she knew she could trust God to do what was best for Eva. One thing Hope had learned for certain over the past fifteen years was that God loved her children more than she ever could. She had to have faith in His unfailing love. Trust Him to do what was best.

She caught her breath at the look of utter joy shining in Rosemary's face as she lifted her chin and accepted her new husband's kiss.

Hank had turned over the church to Gregory, and he and Rosemary were starting an orphanage in Oregon City. So many children reached the end of the Oregon Trail motherless and fatherless. Too often, the children ended up on the streets to fend for themselves. Hank and Rosemary were determined to make a difference.

Hope's gaze shifted to Miss Hannah, who occupied the seat in front of Andy. She could understand her mother-in-law's pride in Hank. There was something special about a child whom God had called to preach the gospel.

Next to her, Aimee made a lovely figure in a gown of rose-colored silk. The sweet-spirited, twenty-six-year-old young woman would have made the perfect preacher's wife. And from the look of adoration on her face when she looked at Gregory, Hope knew Aimee agreed.

Hope's heart went out to the girl. To Gregory, she was a

beloved childhood playmate, a cousin by marriage, someone to protect, tease, love as much as one could love a family member, but he would never, ever fall in love with Aimee.

Hope knew some day Aimee would understand that. She only hoped the girl didn't allow true love to slip through her fingers while she dreamed of the impossible. Next to her, Betsy cradled her newborn son whom she'd named after her pa, Andy. James, her proud husband, slipped his arm about her shoulders and smiled down at his sleeping son.

Hope breathed a contented sigh. She cast a quick glance toward the door. With a gold star pinned to his leather vest, Billy sat, ever watching to make sure law was preserved. He wouldn't have missed the wedding for anything but had made it clear he'd have to sit close to the door in case he was needed. He considered his love of the law to be every bit the calling Gregory's preaching was, and Hope didn't doubt it for a moment. Everyone agreed he was a fine sheriff. And she couldn't have been more proud.

"Can I go outside now, Ma?" Eva's tug at her sleeve brought Hope to her senses. She realized the wedding was over and the bride and groom were being presented as Mr. and Mrs. Hank Riley.

Hope stood with the rest of the congregation. She glanced around, and her heart filled with a sense of contentment. These people represented everything God had brought into her life at a time when she thought life held nothing but heartache for her. He'd brought her the love of a godly man, children who knew and served the Lord. She didn't know what the coming years would bring for her loved ones, but she believed with all of her heart that God had good things planned for the Rileys. Her heart nearly burst with thankfulness.

As if sensing her mood, Andy turned away from the bride and groom and looked at her. She gave him a weepy smile.

He took her hand and pressed it close to his heart. Hope rested her head on his shoulder.

The past fifteen years had brought her more happiness than she'd ever dreamed possible. But as she stood in the midst of her family, hope, stronger than ever, sprang in her heart, and she knew the best years of her life were yet to come.

A Letter To Our Readers

Dear Reader:

In order that we might better contribute to your reading enjoyment, we would appreciate your taking a few minutes to respond to the following questions. We welcome your comments and read each form and letter we receive. When completed, please return to the following:

Fiction Editor
Heartsong Presents
PO Box 719
Uhrichsville, Ohio 44683

. Did you enjoy reading *Everlasting Hope* by Tracey V. Bateman?
❏ Very much! I would like to see more books by this author!
❏ Moderately. I would have enjoyed it more if

_____

_____

_____

. Are you a member of **Heartsong Presents**? ❏ Yes ❏ No
If no, where did you purchase this book? _____

_____

. How would you rate, on a scale from 1 (poor) to 5 (superior),
the cover design? _____

. On a scale from 1 (poor) to 10 (superior), please rate the
following elements.

_____ Heroine	_____ Plot
_____ Hero	_____ Inspirational theme
_____ Setting	_____ Secondary characters

5. These characters were special because?_____
_____
_____

6. How has this book inspired your life?_____
_____
_____

7. What settings would you like to see covered in future
   Heartsong Presents books? _____
_____
_____

8. What are some inspirational themes you would like to see
   treated in future books? _____
_____
_____

9. Would you be interested in reading other **Heartsong
   Presents** titles? ❑ Yes ❑ No

10. Please check your age range:
   ❑ Under 18   ❑ 18-24
   ❑ 25-34   ❑ 35-45
   ❑ 46-55   ❑ Over 55

Name _____
Occupation _____
Address _____
City_____ State_____ Zip_____

Heartsong

HISTORICAL ROMANCE IS CHEAPER BY THE DOZEN!

Any 12 Heartsong Presents titles for only $27.00*

Buy any assortment of twelve *Heartsong Presents* **titles and save 25% off of the already discounted price of $2.97 each!**

*plus $2.00 shipping and handling per order and sales tax where applicable.

HEARTSONG PRESENTS TITLES AVAILABLE NOW:

(If ordering from this page, please remember to include it with the order form.)

Presents

Great Inspirational Romance at a Great Price!

Heartsong Presents books are inspirational romances in contemporary and historical settings, designed to give you an enjoyable, spirit-lifting reading experience. You can choose wonderfully written titles from some of today's best authors like Peggy Darty, Sally Laity, Tracie Peterson, Colleen L. Reece, Debra White Smith, and many others.